There was movement _____ _____ _____ _____
floor.

"Okay," the shooter said. "It's all okay."

Sounds gained momentum and built on one another.

"All right now." The shooter spoke only to himself but didn't know it. "It's fine."

A wall of noise and panic moved in on him. There were screams. The man who had been shot slapped the floor with a flat, open hand. He kicked the table leg with his heel. Silverware went flying across tabletops.

"Mike," the wife whispered. Then she yelled "Mike!" over and over while another woman, a large one in a yellow flower-print sundress, grabbed her purse, put it in the bend of her elbow and started running. She had one hand over her mouth.

The shooter felt vibrations through the floor. He felt them through the soles of his feet.

"Mike!" the woman yelled. "Oh my God Mike oh my God."

The shooter yelled, but no one heard him over the noise and the awakening to the reality of what was going on.

"All right. Okay. All right now," he said.

He fired multiple shots in a line. It was a dotted line that started in the center of the woman in the yellow sundress and led away from her. She went down. Her purse trailed after her. The man next to her was shot in the throat.

It was amazing.

BAD DAY

For The

HOME TEAM

ALEX O'MEARA

ZUMAYA PUBLICATIONS LLC   AUSTIN TX

2010

BAD DAY FOR THE HOME TEAM

© 2010 by Alex O'Meara

ISBN 978-1-936144-36-5

Cover art and design © Chris Cartwright

"Zumaya Publications" and the Zumaya colophon are trademarks of Zumaya Publications LLC, Austin TX.

Look for us online at
http://www.zumayapublications.com

Library of Congress Cataloging-in-Publication Data

O'Meara, Alex.
  Bad day for the home team / Alex O'Meara.
      p. cm.
  ISBN 978-1-936144-36-5 (trade paper : alk. paper) — ISBN 978-1-936144-37-2 (eBook)
    1.   Future life—Fiction. 2.   Murder—Investigation—Fiction. 3.   Self-realization—Fiction. 4.   Psychological fiction.   I. Title.
  PS3615.M43B34 2010
  813'.6—dc22
                                                    2010028335

for Karen O'Meara

If Van Gogh were alive today, I think he'd take a few people with him before he killed himself.

– Sam Tryor

—1—

*I*t just went off, like, *oops*. The first shot hit solid and sent a guy cutting pizza for his son back into a wall.

"Wow," the shooter said. "I'm sorry."

He apologized in the same tone a mother uses when she tells her child the hamster died.

"What was that?" someone said. "What the hell?"

The shooter looked at his gun. A woman went over to the man who had been shot. She looked at the shooter with an expression like the saleslady in the china shop about to say, *You know you have to pay for that now, don't you?* The toddler with them—he couldn't have been more than four—put a bite of pizza into his mouth and looked at the man. He clapped his hands like he was saying *goody-goody gumdrops!*

There was movement.

Chairs scraped against the floor.

"Okay," the shooter said. "It's all okay."

Sounds gained momentum and built on one another.

"All right now." The shooter spoke only to himself but didn't know it. "It's fine."

A wall of noise and panic moved in on him. There were screams. The man who had been shot slapped the

1

floor with a flat, open hand. He kicked the table leg with his heel. Silverware went flying across tabletops.

"Mike," the man's wife whispered. Then she yelled "Mike!" over and over while another woman, a large one in a yellow flower-print sundress, grabbed her purse, put it in the bend of her elbow and started running. She had one hand over her mouth.

The shooter felt vibrations through the floor. He felt them through the soles of his feet.

"Mike!" the woman yelled. "OhmyGodMikeohmy-God."

The shooter yelled, but no one heard him over the noise and the awakening to the reality of what was going on.

"All right. Okay. All right now," he said.

He fired multiple shots in a line. It was a dotted line that started in the center of the woman in the yellow sundress and led away from her. She went down. Her purse trailed after her. The man next to her was shot in the throat.

It was amazing.

A kid in a corduroy baseball cap looked at him. He held his right ear and just stood there with his mouth open. At first he didn't move to protect anyone, not even himself. Then he turned to get out of there and tell someone about it.

"Don't leave." the shooter told him.

He resumed firing. Shell casings dropped to the floor with hollow clinks.

"Don't," he said.

More people fell. Some staggered forward from the impact then fell. Others just sank. It was crazy. The shooter walked a few steps. He looked like his legs had gone to sleep and he wanted to wake them up.

"God, I'm sweating," he said.

He ran for the door to get in front of it, to block it. "No," he said. "Okay. Okay."

He put his arm around the shoulder of the kid who had held his ear.

"Go and sit down now," he said to him gently. "Everybody, listen. I want everybody to just listen."

Everybody huddled in two groups in the corners about twenty feet away. They moved chairs in front of them and held on to table legs for protection. One woman said "Hail, Mary." Another said, "Mike, wake up."

"It's all right now," the shooter assured them.

No one believed him. He'd always had trouble talking in front of groups. He preferred the one-on-one.

"Is there anyone in the back there?" he asked the kid in the baseball cap. "Go check. Go. You."

It took the young man three tries to open the swinging half-door to the kitchen.

"Pull it. Try pulling it. That's the stuff. Good."

There was heavy breathing. Everything in the room was becoming less fuzzy. Strangers looked at one another to confirm what was happening was really happening. The two clumps of people huddled tighter together and looked at the gun. They didn't look at him. He was obscured by the greater reality of the gun.

He looked like he didn't know what to do. He just stood there.

"He's alive," someone screamed.

"No one's back there," the kid said in a twisted yell once he came back from the kitchen. He was still holding his ear. "Can I go now? I'd like to go. Now. I'll just…"

And he left.

The first guy who was shot was still hitting the floor with his hand. It was soft as a whisper. Slap, slap, slap.

The guy with the gun looked out a window with the blinds up. The sunny day continued. The cars passed on Fry Boulevard. The tires made that sizzling sound.

"Do something," said a woman in the corner to her boyfriend. "Do something, Jerry. Look at him."

She wanted him to be a hero. That was a mistake.

Jerry got up and made it only three steps before he was shot in the chest. A smattering of goo hit against the window with a splat. Behind the balls of blood, the shooter saw a man in the parking lot get out of his car. He saw him look at the restaurant window.

"I got to do it," the shooter said.

He braced the gun against his shoulder and kept it low while he walked and fired. People scattered, and a few hit the ground. One man with blond hair and a chain that held his wallet to his belt loop crouched behind the dead woman in the yellow sundress and called for his mother.

The shooter straight-line walked and shot on automatic. It looked very easy. The clip emptied. He reloaded and continued until he was about five feet from the wall.

"Oh, damn," he said, like he'd forgotten to mail something.

He turned around to face the other group of people and shot a college girl as she ran for the door. She wore a T-shirt, bathing suit bottom and flip-flops. When she fell, the flip-flops slapped against her heel one last time and that was it.

People dove under tables. They kicked and hurled their bodies into tight places. The scratched along the Mexican tiled floor. It was very fast. Everyone moved very fast.

A woman off to the side noticed the shooter's face. She saw that his eyes were absolutely huge.

"Hot bullets," he said to no one in particular.

He stopped at a table and poured a Pepsi on the top of the gun, and on his hand. He stopped firing and watched a man behind the wheel of a car in the parking lot. The man's hand slipped along the gearshift as he put it in reverse. He was horrified, looking into the restaurant, but he was still a careful driver: He checked his mirrors before he backed up.

He was sure to call someone. They would come soon.

The shooter adjusted his grip on the gun. The woman watched his knuckles carefully. She saw them turn from white to red when he relaxed his hands. She saw them tense and go white again and held her breath.

He gripped the gun and sucked in as hard as a long jumper before a leap. Then he just went everywhere with the gun. The barrel flying hot, shots opened along the wall, glass shattered, an upper arm got all chewed up, and the cash register got hit. Its drawer popped open like a tongue. The shooter raised his foot high and kicked it hard. Nickels, dimes, quarters and pennies sprinkled down. Bills fluttered. They looked absurd in the smoke, and weirder still when they landed. One $20 bill soaked up the blood on a hole in the college girl's forehead.

"He's a mess," Jerry's girlfriend said. She was on the floor holding him as he spasmed. His shirt was reddened wounds. "This is a mess." The woman stroked his head and muttered. "Jerry, do something. Do something, Jerry, do something."

A girl noticed the shooter looked tired. Weary was the word, she thought.

He raised the gun to fire and everyone tensed, but then he didn't shoot. He dropped to a relaxed position. He thrust his arm with the gun forward, like he was trying to shake it off. Then he did, and the gun clattered to the ground, empty. He looked around, picked up an iced tea and took a long gulp.

"I always liked iced tea."

No one moved when he spoke. A lot of people kept their eyes on the gun, even though it was on the floor. For a few moments now, everyone had been quiet and still. It was like the silence when no one can think of what to say at a party.

"Looks like a bad day for the home team," the shooter said.

He pulled a pistol from his back pocket and put the barrel in his mouth.

"Oh, yes, finally, you fuck," a voice said.

He looked toward the ceiling where an overhead fan spun slowly. He took the gun from his mouth and aimed it around. But he didn't shoot.

"Come on," someone said.

Ten feet away, a black woman stood up, walked to the door and said, "Let me. I'll do it if you can't."

"No, that's fine," he said. "Thank you. I can take care of it. I can."

"All right, then," the woman said.

The other people started moving.

"Don't," he said quietly. "Don't move."

It was so sunny out. It was a good day. He put the tip of the gun to his mouth.

"Bad day for the home team," he said. "I'm sorry about all this."

He pulled the trigger.

—2—

*I*t was the middle of the afternoon. My brother Nick had just woken up from a nap. His house was musty and hazy. He was talking on the phone with someone named Charlie. They were talking about a shooting at the Pizza Man restaurant.

I heard "Pizza Man," and I knew I was dead. I couldn't remember a thing about it, but I knew. I felt calm.

"Do you think Sam was there?" Nick said to Charlie.

I stood behind the easy chair, off to the side, dead. When I say dead, I don't mean like "I'm in trouble" or "I'm very tired." I mean as in deceased. As in not living. I said the word over and over to myself until it sank in and lost all meaning.

My body felt the same way as a house when the power goes out, still and oddly peaceful. There was no hum of activity coming from inside me. I was freed from the simplest physical effort. I was not breathing. My heart was not beating. Gravity was not pulling on those extra twenty pounds that made it a little tough for me to get around. I had no aches or pains. My eyes did not blink. I did not float. I stood there, and the chair went right through where my stomach would have been.

Nick was still on the phone, listening to Charlie. He lit a cigarette. I knew he wanted to quit. I knew he never would. I hadn't been able to. I wondered if, now I was dead, that meant I had finally quit. I didn't know the rules about smoking after death. I didn't know the rules about being dead.

Nick asked Charlie if he thought I was in the Pizza Man. Then he listened to him answer. I thought about my situation.

Let me tell you about being dead. There was no bright light to move toward or away from. There was no organ music. I did not see my great-aunt Betty or meet Abraham Lincoln. I did not see gates, pearly or otherwise, and I did not see Jesus. If I had seen Him, I would have asked Him how I got where I was.

I had no idea how I died. That made me uneasy.

If I could start from my life and work forward maybe, I thought, I could figure it out. But I didn't know anything about my life. My power-outage calm turned into a slow panic. Hell of a day, I thought. First I die, then I lose my life.

I took stock of what I did know. I was at my brother Nick's, house. My name was Sam Tryor, I was fifty-two years old, and I lived in Sierra Vista, Arizona. I was wearing tan pants, black shoes, white socks, a white short-sleeved shirt and a tie from Miami Beach. I was a lousy dresser. Was I married? Nope. I looked at my left hand, and I didn't have a wedding ring. What I did have was a splitting headache and a nagging feeling that, in addition to my being dead, something was very wrong.

"No," Nick said into the phone, "Sam didn't drink. I mean, not a lot. Not in the middle of the afternoon."

That triggered something. One time I got really drunk on tequila, woke up the next morning and realized I had blacked out. I asked my friends what I did the night before. It turned out all I did was drum on pillows and pots and pans while insisting over and over that I was the Tito Puente of the bongos.

I wanted to ask Nick what I did the night before, about my life before. Was I left- or right-handed? What did I do for a living? Was I a cat or a dog person? Was I cool?

I sat next to Nick on the couch.

"Boo!" I said. "Boo, Nicky! It's me, Sam. Boo! Hello?"

Nothing. I waved my arms and yelled as loud as I could. No reaction. Nick said to Charlie on the phone, "Yes, Sam was in the army. I don't remember his rank."

Yes, yes! I had been in the army! Great. I loved the army. The army taught me I was not unique, not special, not creative, not even interesting. I remembered. And from the first day I joined, the army loved me.

They gave me a skills aptitude test when I enlisted. They wanted to see if I was better suited to be a marksman or a cook. I filled in the fifty little circles for the fifty little questions, and the sergeant called his lieutenant over. The lieutenant said he'd never seen anything like it. They double-checked my answers then made me take the test over. Same results. Amazing. The test said I was best suited to be a US Army private.

They told me to take a different, more detailed test that measured basically the same thing. The army had lots of tests. They got the same results. I was born to be a US Army private. The test also showed that I thought of myself as nothing more than what I was. They said I was "spectacularly normal" and that made me "profoundly malleable and psychologically flexible." They said I was "uniquely incapable of considering abstraction." They slotted me for CIA training.

I remembered something. Good.

Nick hung up the phone. He decided to go to the scene of the shooting at the Pizza Man and find out what was going on. He headed for the bathroom to splash a little water on his face, brush his teeth, floss.

While Nick was in the bathroom, I saw a photo of him and me on the wall. Every year we took a new photo of us together on Nick's birthday. It was a tradition. I stared at the photo. I looked like a felon. I looked like I lacked confidence. My nose was too big. My arms hung stupidly at my sides. My grin looked fake and forced. I was slumping. My skin was blotchy. A picture for posterity, and I stood there looking more pathetic than a day-shift stripper.

Nick radiated success and confidence. He was proud. He beamed. He looked like whoever saw that picture should send him a check as a thank-you for the privilege of seeing that picture. My brother, I remembered, was a millionaire.

I saw my reflection in the glass of the photo. There wasn't a mark on me. I must have died of a heart attack. It was better than dying in a pizza place. No one in their right mind wants to die in a pizza place. I looked like the kind of guy who would die of a heart attack. I hoped that was it. I wanted it to be a massive coronary infarction occlusion.

My father died of a heart attack. He was standing in his skivvies at the open refrigerator at two a.m., reaching for another Falstaff, and he keeled over, stiffer than a Presbyterian at Mardi Gras before he even hit the floor. For the first time, I wanted to take after the old man. I wanted to have been standing there one minute and—wham!—kissing the linoleum the next. Something told me that wasn't the case.

Nick was convinced I had been shot in the Pizza Man.

I knew that because I could read his mind. The hits kept coming. I was hot-wired into his brain. I thought about the blackout when he mentioned booze. I thought about the army only after he mentioned it. His photos and his house sent me off remembering things. It was like he was a radio receiver, and I was getting all my information through him.

I poked my head into the bathroom. Nick looked into the mirror for a long time. He wanted to get going, he wanted to take steps, but he wasn't ready. One more cigarette, then he would be ready. He didn't know for sure that I was dead, but he had a feeling about it.

He lit a Camel Light and looked at himself in the bathroom mirror. I had no idea he spent so much time looking at himself. He flicked his cigarette ash into the sink. He leaned forward and stared deep into his own eyes. He thought about the first time he lost his mind. He wondered if he might be losing it again now.

For seventeen months, Nick did not leave his house and did not say a word. He ordered his food, movies, laundry, dry cleaning, booze and whatever else he needed over the internet. To get out of his depression, he set about reinventing himself.

Even though he wasn't much of a drinker, drinking seemed like a good idea to him. So, for a few months Nick drank. A lot. Then he stopped. He realized he wasn't a drunk.

Then he went on a health kick. Truth be told, I liked him better when he drank. He put a treadmill in the corner of the basement, started running every day, weighed his food before each meal and dropped seventy-five pounds. Then he stopped.

For three months, he watched satellite TV. For a month, he was busy with his divorce. After that, for four months, he became obsessed with tracking down every single person from his childhood—teachers, coaches, friends, neighbors from Detroit, you name it. He sent money to some, wrote long letters to others and had cybersex with three, including his fifth-grade teacher, Mrs. Freidkin. Then he stopped.

He taught himself Spanish, but because he wasn't talking to anyone, it was only in his head. He read the *World Book Encyclopedia*. In his basement, he constructed an incredibly precise model of the entire borough of Brooklyn. It was while he was putting the finishing touches on Montgomery Clift's gravesite in the Quaker Cemetery in Prospect Park that his mind came back to him. It returned like it was nothing more than a lost cat that had finally found its way home.

The moment he glued the plastic ivy onto Monty Clift's grave, Nick recognized something important about himself. It was a quality I possessed and he always envied me for. The army thought I was uniquely gifted because of it. Here's what it was:

I was average height, a little over average weight, average smarts. I wasn't particularly gifted or unique. I was not sensitive or charming. I knew nothing about wine and had no desire to see the Cathedral at Chartres. I had no great enthusiasm to change the world, to save or serve the needs of people, to save or serve the whales or stray animals. I did not want to save others, or even myself, from any vices. I was not blessed with special insight about God or the world. Politicians were just sons of bitches who bored me. Nick had one child to lug him to the grave, but if she didn't want the job, that was fine with him. I had no children to carry me or carry on for me, and that was fine. Everything, for me, was always fine.

What made me special was that I knew I was nothing special. That day, Nick realized the same thing about himself. He was just Nick. He always would be Nick. He gave up on any notion of reinventing himself as a drinker, as an athlete, as anything other than who he was. It took him seventeen months and losing his mind to realize who he was, but he did it.

"I am nuts," Nick said out loud to his miniature version of Brooklyn that day. "I am bolts. That's who I am. That has never changed. That will never change."

The morning he broke his silence, I came over and, like I did every day, made him breakfast of eggs over hard, rye toast and sausages. We sat in his kitchen, and just like the previous seventeen months, he was stone silent. He went by me like I was a ghost.

When he was done with the eggs but before he got to the sausages, the first thing he said was, "We should buy a Ford Fairlane. We should retrace our steps from when we came out here from Detroit. We can see where we went wrong."

"You're a weird fuckin' guy, Nick," I said. "Weird fuckin'."

"Your mother."

"Hey, Nick," I said.

"Yeah."

"Shut the fuck up already."

⊙━◎

Now Nick stood at the bathroom sink getting ready to leave for the Pizza Man, smoking and thinking. As he did, every one of my dead synapses crackled with life.

Nick spent one last moment checking himself out in the mirror.

I am nuts. I am bolts. I need logistics, he thought.

That's how he learned to dance. He was eight years old, and he used those black footsteps—the kind with the heel and the toe set out on paper. The concept of rhythm and placement went from a mishmash blur to clear reality for him, thanks to an easy-to-follow dia-gram that let him put his feet on the feet provided.

13

I, on the other hand, was more of a creative thinker. I was a self-starter. I needed no such instructions. I made up the rules for myself and went with my gut. I was a rebel, an idea man

Actually, that's a lie. Except for the few morsels I learned through Nick, I still had no idea about who I was before I died. My normalcy didn't necessarily mean I wasn't a success. I could have cured cancer, won the Nobel Peace Prize and been married at one time to a Norwegian supermodel. Or, I could have been a surly mouth-breather who drank 40s and mainlined heroin every day of my adult life. I didn't care either way. I just wanted to find out.

"The point is to find out," Nick said to his reflection in the bathroom. "To find out, you go where someone knows. Who knows? The police. So, go where it happened. The scene of the crime."

He walked purposefully into the living room and grabbed his car keys. He stopped as his hand grasped the doorknob. *Everything will be all right. Nothing ever changes.* Even as he thought it, Nick knew somewhere inside—deep inside—that by the time he got back to his house later, everything would be changed.

I knew it, too.

In the car, Nick went over what he knew: *Sam might be at a restaurant where a shooting took place. Charlie'd said, "It could be Sam." What could be Sam? Do not over-think this. Does this mean Sam's dead? Am I losing my mind? Again? It was different last time. This feels different. Did Sam get shot in a restaurant? Would he? Could he? Charlie's an ex-cop. Sam.*

As kids we would say, "What would I do without you?" We would plan our reaction to each other's death, the way brothers do. The old Us Against the World. There were times when I wanted him to be dead so I could be pitied. They would let me out of school for months. The dumb

stuff you think as a kid. I should do something here. Sam is dead. Is he?

At first, after I knew I was dead, there was the sensation of floating on an ocean of calm. Then, when I couldn't remember how I died, a little island of unease appeared and I was floating on more of a lake of calm. By the time I realized my entire life was wiped from my memory, the calm was a puddle and the unease had grown into a continent. I was dead, but I was not gone.

It was obvious: I was a ghost.

I had never seen a ghost, but when I was a kid I loved to take a flashlight under the covers and read ghost stories. I remembered them all.

On March 13, 1956, Mildred Ann Reynolds was killed in her car in Avard, Oklahoma. Her murder was never solved. It is said that, occasionally, Ms. Reynolds likes to come in to Vina Rae's Grill wearing the same green dress she was killed in. She never orders anything, and she doesn't make eye contact with anyone.

Does Mildred Ann hear people debate between tuna in oil or water in the Safeway? As she comes in contact with people as she goes around trying to find her killer, does she instantly know the kind of backpack each one of those people carried in the third grade? Is she looking for her killer? If they solve the crime, will she go away?

Is it a hard-and-fast rule that ghosts are on a mission?

One block after Nick turned onto Fry Boulevard to go to the Pizza Man, his car got trapped in a swarm of police and ambulance sirens. They were all around us one moment and gone the next. For that second inside the pulsing lights, it sounded like the blitz. Nick watched the red, amber and blue beating lights take off down the street in front of him. They were going where he was going. He lit another cigarette off the one he was smoking.

It wasn't a heart attack. My gut told me I hadn't been that lucky. It told me I had been gunned down in the Pizza Man.

If they solved my murder, I wondered, would I go away? Was I there to solve the shooting at the Pizza Man, like Mildred Ann was sent to solve her murder? Was that my mission?

"Nicky," I said one more time, "it's me! Boo!"

Nothing.

Some ghost. My mother's words came back to haunt me—I was an underachiever.

The Pizza Man was just up ahead.

—3—

*T*he next thing I knew, I was with an enormous black guy driving down Fry Boulevard. He was tapping his foot on the accelerator, making his huge Cadillac lurch like a Tilt-A-Whirl gone bad. He kept repeating, "Fuck. Fuck. Fuck."

"Come on, now," he said. "Let's go here. Jesus, people. No timing."

He had a gun. It was in a holster and poked out from under his suit jacket.

He was yelling his head off.

Then I saw his badge. The guy's name was Walter Perry. He was a Sierra Vista detective. A lieutenant. Before that, he had been a cop in Baltimore. I knew where he went to grammar school. I knew that in the third grade he carried a *Six Million-Dollar Man* lunchbox with a Scooby Doo thermos. It really pissed him off that the thermos and lunchbox didn't match. I knew the name of Perry's pet turtle when he was seven years old.

It was Poke, as in slow.

There was a movie with Christopher Walken called *The Dead Zone*. He played a guy who woke up from a coma after five years with the ability to tell the future when he shook hands with someone. He would get all freaked out and go into a trance. Then he would set out to change the future if it was horrible. Being a Stephen King story, it was usually horrible. Christopher Walken's character was confused and conflicted because of the global and moral implications that arose from trying to change the future.

I was confused and conflicted from the stress of trying to know the past. Being a ghost was proving to be way over my head. I wanted to pick up a pen and make a list of what was good about my ghostly powers and what was bad. I wondered if Superman had wanted to do the same thing when he was a kid figuring it all out. Under *Good* he would put flying, superhuman strength and x-ray vision. Under *Bad* he would put having to be Clark Kent, not being able to hook up with Lois Lane and kryptonite, which he probably underlined four times.

Underneath *Good* I'd put my ability to read thoughts, which was pretty cool, and the ability to know things about a person, especially about their past, when I came into contact with them. I knew parts of Perry's past, and I also felt like I knew Perry instantaneously. Under *Bad*, I'd put that I jumped from place to place and person to person with no warning, that I couldn't remember my own life, and that I had no control over my mind-reading. When I tried to read Perry's thoughts, I got nothing. The information just came unbidden, unstructured and unfiltered.

For instance, I knew that Perry was going to the Pizza Man because a cop named Raphael Cortez was losing control of the situation there. I knew that because I knew Perry had been at home when he heard the scanner traffic. It was Cortez and Bev, the dispatcher. They were failing to negotiate the chaos of the shooting. He got in his car and drove to the scene. He dragged his thoughts over the possibilities. He was always prepared for the worst.

He had three police scanners. Scanners were Perry's way of remaining connected to his work. As a cop, that meant being connected to his life. The pops and hisses were more than a comfort to him. The grating crackle was an umbilical to his very being.

His home scanner was in the kitchen, just above the sink and under the spice rack. His wife would turn it down when he was away. When he came home he went right to it and cranked it up. It didn't matter much because his wife was rarely around. She was usually out on a date.

He carried a handheld scanner in case of power outages. His third scanner was under the dash in his Cadillac, a 1973 Eldorado. Perry stood six feet, five inches and topped the scale at two hundred-forty-five pounds, and, man, he loved his big-ass Caddy with the 550-cubic-inch engine block. Everyone had their idea of art, and for Perry, art came out of Detroit in the 1970s

I knew Perry didn't yell or use words like *dickstump* at home, at work or in the grocery store. It was only when he was going down the road, in his car, with the world in his sights, that he became a freak. He once spent five minutes cursing out a nun on a Sunday for not using her turn signal. He once yelled at a guy with a broken foot who was gimping slowly in front of his car, "Hurry up or I'll take your other leg." And he meant it.

"Hey! Hey, dickhead!" Perry yelled as we went down Fry Boulevard. "Look where you're going. This isn't a carnival here. This is the real thing. Come on, come on, come on. I don't have all day. Ralph might be in trouble, people. Let's move."

Perry wasn't bashful about his size. He stood straight with his shoulders back and his head held high, just like his five-foot, eight-inch-tall daddy told him to.

That's about all I knew about Walter Perry at the moment the police scanner in the Cadillac went quiet. Perry slowed down as he drove along Fry. He tapped the scanner with his finger, swerved into the next lane and cut off a pickup truck.

Dead scanner, he thought. Not a good thing.

He got nervous when things got quiet.

Perry thought about when he was a fresh cop back in Baltimore. Three years out of the academy, and he was so eager, so tightly wound. Every day, every call for him was going to be *the thing*. The *bad thing*. He knew it. He felt marked. Pulling someone over for a traffic ticket, he was such a mass of tension it was amazing he could even move his legs to walk over to the driver's-side window. He saw buildings in peripheral vision down to being able to tell whether the blinds in the windows were up or down. He memorized locations, angles, weather patterns, the play of shadows in the trees. He would voice narration of the scene in the voice of Walter Winchell introducing an episode of *The Untouchables*.

Walter Perry was a good cop. He'd never had to unholster his gun until that day at 2:53 on a hot side street when the white Dodge cruised through a stop-light then idled roughly, waiting for him

Winchell never narrated a story where Perry was the hero. He always put Perry in the wrong place at the wrong time.

Perry thought about the day Walter Winchell called it right.

A sweaty, stupid junkie in Baltimore held up a liquor store with a shotgun. The dumb kid could barely hold the big barrel horizontal. The guy behind the counter handed him all the money in a paper bag, but the kid stayed there thinking about whatever it was junkies think about when they rob people. At last, the kid said, "Bushmills. I want some of that. My old man drank that shit."

"Isn't that sweet," the man behind the counter said.

"Don't fuck with me about my old man!" *Bam!* The display of airline liquor bottles took a direct shotgun blast.

The man in the liquor store practically threw the kid his bottle.

"Put it in a bag," the junkie said. "Cops see me with a bottle they're going to hassle me, man. See? I know stuff."

He did like the kid said.

"Okay, now. Yeah." The kid looked around jerkily. "All right. I'm gone."

The kid turned to the door and saw Perry peering in. They startled one another. Perry went for it, but he was a moment off. The blast of pellets and glass caught him in the neck and face. He swore he saw debris rushing at him in slow motion, and if he hadn't tucked his head down, he'd be blind.

The kid rushed through the hole where the door's glass had been a second before, and Perry tackled him and hugged him so tight blood squirted from the holes in his face.

In the emergency room, Perry counted the metal pellets and glass slivers as fifty-two of them were dropped from tweezers into a metal bowl. Fifty-two cards in a deck. Fifty-two weeks in a year. When fifty-two American hostages were captured in Iran, Perry believed there was a pattern at work that included him.

He may have been on to something. I was fifty-two years old when I died.

Perry left Baltimore looking like he'd survived a bad case of chicken pox. He went west, to Arizona. There were no secrets in the city, he said. Too many people regarded him as "the shot cop." His driving got worse. He was worn out. He spent all that time waiting for the thing only to be proven right. In Sierra Vista, not only did the thing never happen, nothing ever happened. It was a small hick town, and for Perry, it was perfect. Perry's Walter Winchell narration was now only a private joke with himself. Sometimes, he would forget and narrate out loud.

"It's cop stuff," he would say to the citizen who called him on it. "You wouldn't understand. Cop stuff. Give me your license so I don't have to shoot you."

A Subaru came to a sudden stop at a yellow light in front of Perry on Fry Boulevard and yanked him out of his reverie. The girl in the car got very busy looking at her lips in the rearview.

"Hey, you fuckwad, asswipe piece of shit," Perry yelled. "I'm driving here. Call in, Ralph. Call in."

Jesus. Why are blondes always driving red cars? When are they going to learn they look better in Jeeps?

His thoughts were trying to cover up the awful, empty nothing coming from the scanner. Perry was only five blocks away from the Pizza Man. Five blocks and two unsynchronized lights away from the crime scene, and neither he nor I had any idea what was happening. All we had was a bad feeling.

He saw a car with a bumper sticker that said: THERE'S NOTHING IN THIS TRUCK WORTH YOUR LIFE.

He sat at the light and looked into the blonde's rearview eyes. He wished he had sirens and a gun turret mounted on the roof of his car.

One block farther, and he hit the next red.

He had good reason to be worried about what was happening at the Pizza Man.

—4—

I found myself in the parking lot in front of the Pizza Man. The scene of the crime was some kind of scene, all right.

I watched a woman crawl up—literally—Patrolman Raphael Cortez. Whether he was named for the explorer, the artist or the Neil Young song, he looked nothing like any of them as he stood with this woman scaling him.

I didn't ask what I was doing there. As a soldier, I was taught you go where you are sent, you do not ask questions, you do not ask why, you just go, and if told to do something, you do what you are told. Everything has a reason. Even if it doesn't have a reason, it has a reason. I understood. I allowed the information to just flow through me like the floodwaters flowed through Johnstown and chose to concentrate on soaking up what I could.

Cortez watched the Pizza Man. He had one hand on the radio transmitter while the other moved to his gun, then away from it, then back. It looked to me like he was deciding if he should take it out and shoot something. He looked like a child armed with two fingers in front of the mirror playing the final scene from *High Noon*. He looked a little goofy.

The woman had made it to Cortez's back, and her feet were completely off the ground. She had turned his radio off when she climbed him. He didn't know that, and I couldn't tell him. He stood there, supporting the woman's weight, and tried to serve and protect. They don't show you this stuff on TV.

"Hey. Hey, you fuck," the woman piggybacking Cortez said. "Get in there. Call for backup or whatever it is you do. I could be shot here."

Come on, I thought, say it. It's too perfect. You have to say, "Get off my back, lady." But he didn't.

"Someone will be along shortly, ma'am," Cortez said. "Remain with the car between yourself and the location."

I sound like some sort of robot, he thought.

"You sound like a robot!" the woman said. "Do they teach you to say that in cop school or something?"

I looked around. It was a beautiful day. I looked across the street. I saw a boy, no more than eight years old, who had wandered away from what looked like a big party going on in Veteran's Park. He was walking with a balloon. A yellow one.

It was nice to see something normal. It cheered me up. The kid jerked the balloon down and watched it drift back up. I forgot about the woman smeared with blood who wept and moaned about the carnage and the lawsuit she and her lawyer would bring, so help her God.

The boy's mother yelled for him, and his head snapped in her direction. He looked like every summoned child—guilty, interrupted and scared. The string slithered out of his hand.

I wished I could have gone and spent some time with that kid. It looked like a good to deal to me. It looked a damned sight better than the hand Cortez had been dealt.

"Ma'am," Cortez said, "if you could please get off of me."

The woman suddenly swung her purse over his shoulder and hit him in the chest with it. That had to hurt. He didn't react. She was gurgling an amalgam of Spanish and English, speaking so wetly and quickly Cortez couldn't figure out what she was saying in either language, even though he spoke both. She swung again. There was something hard in that purse. A gun? A rock? Whatever it was, it hit him in the elbow, and it must have hurt like a son of a bitch.

"Just ease it down now," he said through gritted teeth. "You don't want this."

The woman slid off him and lay on the ground at his feet.

"Officer, do you need some help?" a woman—a very beautiful young woman—said.

Her name was Sarah Tilly. She was a reporter for the local paper. She had expected to see a scene of unspeakable carnage and was let down to find just a woman belting the hell out of a cop.

"I'm from the *Herald*," Sarah said, walking closer to Cortez and taking out her notepad and her pen. "What's happening here? On the scanner, it sounded like something."

Cortez looked at Sarah like she had dropped out of the sky. The woman who had been on him also turned her attention to Sarah. She gently wrapped one of her hands around Sarah's ankle. Then she moved it up her calf and her thigh. Sarah didn't move.

"Am I hit?" the woman moaned. "Tell me. Look. Did he get me? That motherfucker in there. Did he get me? I see blood."

"Officer, what should I do here?" Sarah asked.

25

The woman started to climb Sarah. If she hadn't been covered in blood, I would have sworn this was part of a sorority rush stunt. She was up to Sarah's waist and was ascending her like she was the only refuge in a rising flood.

"She's pretty high up on me," Sarah said. "What should I do?"

Cortez watched the two women entwine vertically. In the middle of this slow weirdness, he looked at Sarah and thought, She's my kind of woman, prim and sexy. Redhead. Nice. Looks like she's got that business-suit-over-hot-lingerie thing going on.

"Hey!" Sarah yelled at Cortez. "Kid! Can you get this woman off of me?"

"Just bitch-slap her down, lady," he said. "I got problems of my own."

The woman curled down off Sarah and settled onto the hot tar of the parking lot, where she played with a pebble and muttered her brand of Spanish.

"What sort of problems?" Sarah asked Cortez.

"Remain with the car between yourself and the restaurant, please," Cortez said. "There's a guy in there who may have shot some people. That's the situation. So, do I stay here and wait for backup? I mean, where is somebody?"

"Nobody calls," the woman on the ground murmured, "nobody writes, nobody cares."

"Or do I go in because he may shoot more people?" Cortez said. "There may be hostages. There may be wounded. It may be a false alarm that doesn't call for police action, and this crazy person playing with the rock here could be, I don't know, a terrorist. You know?"

"At least you have a gun," Sarah said, fingering her notebook and pen, which to her was very little to be armed with. She looked across the street at Veteran's

Park. There were ten people staring dumb-mouthed. They collectively thought, Freak show.

I couldn't have agreed more.

"Do you think," Sarah said, "we look silly standing here like this?"

❦

I saw Perry pull into the parking lot. He looked at Cortez and Sarah. Then he looked across the street and saw the crowd. He saw they were a secure distance from the scene. Their faces were set in concentration. They leaned slightly forward. They were involved, but they were safe.

The intensity of a crime can be inferred by the size and attitude of the crowd. This was what shot through Perry's mind. At a fender-bender you see people point, compare stories, render judgments, sometimes laugh in relief. At a serious crime scene, no one talks, fathers hold their children tightly, people shield one another, like they did on the grassy knoll at Kennedy's assassination.

The crowd across from the Pizza Man was mute and tense.

Perry drove right toward Ralph, Sarah and me. Then a guy came running out of the Pizza Man. Cortez pulled back the hammer on his gun. The guy wasn't stopping. Cortez wasn't saying anything. Perry imagined all the possibilities—the man dropping, the man pulling out a weapon, Cortez shooting, the screaming.

Before any of that could happen, though, he drove his car right up to Cortez and me.

"Ralph," Perry said softly. "Put the gun away. We're all okay here. Turn your radio on, Ralph. Good boy."

The man from the restaurant—this poor guy who had guns pulled twice on him today when all he wanted was lunch—stopped running, looked at the gun Cortez had aimed at him, then looked back to the restaurant like he thought he might be safer there.

Perry got out of his Caddy.

"Sir," Perry said, turning to the man, his voice firm and professional. "Sir, put your hands on the top of your head. Clasp them together. Slow and easy. We're all calm. We're all thinking of nothing but stopping what we're doing and being friendly to one another. Ralph, now that your gun is away..."

Cortez looked at his gun like someone had planted it in his hand.

"...call in for backup and medical while we straighten this out. Now might be a good time, Ralph."

Cortez relaxed his arms and holstered his gun. He was relieved being told what to do.

He turned his radio back on. He acted like a cop again. His voice was sure, clipped and steady when he told Bev, "Send backup. Eleven-twenty-three Fry Boulevard. Repeat, Eleven-twenty-three Fry, the Pizza Man restaurant. Possible shooting."

Perry, who hadn't even considered unholstering his own gun, walked up to the man from the restaurant. The man stood there with his hands on his head.

"Damn, you're almost as big as me," Perry said, putting a hand on his shoulder.

The minute Perry touched him, the big guy sagged and started crying.

"It's...It...is...real bad...in there. All...all...all shot up. Oh, it's bad."

"All shot. How many?"

"Many."

"Is there someone in there with a gun now? Are they being held?"

"He's dead. They're dead. He's dead. He's dead."

"Go over to the car, and Ralph will help you out. It's going to be okay. Go on, now."

As Perry looked toward the front door of the Pizza Man, Walter Winchell was yapping his head off at him.

He calmed himself.

"I'm going to check it out, Ralph," he said.

"You want my gun?"

"I have a gun. They gave me a gun, too, Ralph."

"You're a great cop," Cortez said. "And a good man."

Remembering the liquor store in Baltimore, Perry didn't put his face in front of the glass door of the restaurant. His gun was still in its holster, though one of his hands rested on it. He opened the door quickly and stepped in. He saw piles of people, and he couldn't speak.

When I saw it, I knew I had been there when it happened. It looked different, though. It looked the way a house you once lived in looks when you visit it years later—small, reduced. No specifics came back, but I knew I had been there.

The carnage was total, Winchell said to Perry.

"Shut up," Perry said. "Shut the fuck up." He yelled to Cortez, "We got people down. We need everything and everyone we can get. Now. This is bad."

"Oh, my God," a woman screamed from the floor inside the restaurant, kicking to move herself toward a corner.

"I'm Lieutenant Perry, Sierra Vista Police. Help will be here momentarily."

"This is a mess," Sarah said from behind Perry. "This is such a mess. God. Look."

A few moments later, it was like everyone in Sierra Vista began arriving at the Pizza Man. Cars and trucks with sirens going started pulling into the parking lot. Police had their guns drawn and were, for some reason, looking up. Firemen in flame-retardant gear, ambulance drivers and EMTs scrambled from their vehicles with plastic bags of fluid and stretchers. They were spreading out everywhere. Radio traffic filled the air with voices talking and awaiting further instructions.

"This is what we train for, boys," a fireman lugging an oxygen tank said. "This is it, now. Right now. This."

Police swarmed over the place. They wore vests and gripped their guns with two hands like they were trying to keep the metal from vibrating. Then, along with Perry and Sarah, they started to move into the cool, dark restaurant sideways, all the time looking and pointing everywhere at once. They propped the doors open. They pointed their hands filled with guns every which way. People inside started screaming. Down on the floor, they twisted, trying to get away from the muzzles, from the memory of guns and bullets.

"It's all right," Perry said. "It's secure. All secure. Help these people."

He looked around. He tried to memorize as much as possible. He thought about how the scene would be categorized by officers, investigators, medical personnel and reporters quoting details. This was his chance to see it pure.

Sarah stood next to him. He took long notice of the notebook in her hand.

"You need to be out of here, Miss."

Sarah looked at a sharp piece of bloody bone on a tabletop. She'd seen dead bodies before, but this was different. The gore on the bone was gooey. It was making her sick.

"I'm staying," she said.

"Miss, please. We have work to do."

"So do I."

"This is a crime scene," Perry said patiently. "If you are here then you alter the crime scene and that alters our investigation, the physics of it. It's a cause-and-effect thing. Very technical."

"I have a First Amendment right to be here," Sarah said. "Freedom of the press. It's in the Constitution. Very technical."

They stood looking at one another.

"So," Sarah said, "what happened?"

"Bill," Perry said, grabbing an officer coming into the restaurant, "escort this nice woman out of here. Thank you."

Sarah tried to look outraged, but she was grateful to be getting out. She had her story. She felt sick, anyway.

The guy who did the shooting was lying on his left side. Perry figured him for the shooter because there was no one near him. Then he saw a gun under his open right hand, and he was sure.

He knelt and felt for a pulse. He saw the man's tan pants, his black belt, white short-sleeved shirt with a Sears label, white socks and black shoes. He brushed his fingers on the man's hair, feeling for the hum in his brain, for its residual thoughts to come through to him so the effort of dissection, the awful picking apart of the man's life to answer "Why?" could be avoided. Perry wanted the two of them to communicate before the others came in.

He noticed the man's tie. It had on it the image of a naked woman who had caught a large aqua-colored fish, grinning and wearing sunglasses.

You have a sense of humor. If you want to say something to me, you better say it now because we don't have much time here, pal, Perry thought. Were you having a bad day, is that it? You sick, crazy in the head? Wife leave you? You can tell me. I'm right here. Right here for you.

"Perry, what have you got over there?" the Sierra Vista Chief of Police, Archibald Samson, said from the door. "That the guy?"

There was a missing wedge of skull at the top left of his head, but his face was intact. Perry looked at the

31

man's open blue eyes and at his face, and noticed he had shaved that day.

He noticed that *I* had shaved that day. He saw *my* face. The top left of *my* head had been shot away.

Perry's wrong, I thought. There was no way.

Then why was there a gun under my right hand?

I'd wanted to know, I had told myself, either way, I just wanted to know. Now I knew. But why would I do something like this?

Oh, God, I thought, Nicky. How was I going to tell him? Then I remembered I wasn't going to, someone else would.

"This is bad," Perry said to my body. "What you did was bad. You should be ashamed."

I was ashamed, but not by what I did. Strangely, I felt no remorse, even if Perry was right and I did do it. I was only ashamed of what Nick would think.

—*5*—

Some ghosts haunt places, others haunt people. On May 12, 1905, in Stillwater, Florida, a family of four was murdered by their father. After he took an axe to his three children and his wife while they slept upstairs, he hanged himself in the living room.

Years later, the house became a museum of the massacre. The owners gave tours, and for a price, anyone who wanted to have an encounter with a ghost could stay overnight.

The sheriff who investigated the killings said he was visited by the spirits of two of the murdered girls. The haunting continued until the day the father was laid to rest in an unmarked grave. Relatives of the murdered children swore to the local newspaper that they felt the children and the father close by them in the days following the crime. They sensed their presence strongest in the house where it happened, but they were with them wherever they went as well. They said it was like they were being followed.

Putting the stories and letters together and making a timeline years later, a parapsychologist said it looked like the ghost, or ghosts, didn't haunt a place. Rather, they bounced from one person to another in the days

after the murders. He said it looked like the ghosts visited several people at the murder scene, then some at the
police station and others at the morgue.

No one ever found out why the father killed his
family.

◦━◦

I was next to Nick. He stood on the outside of the tape-
line that circled the Pizza Man. No one had told him
yet. When he wasn't wondering if I were dead or not, he
thought about the Ford Fairlane and when we came
out to Arizona.

It was 1964. We drove thirty-six hours straight
from Detroit. We were stunned and overwhelmed by the
yucca and desert scrub. We told each other we'd see
snow only in postcards from now on. We were going to
live the lives we longed for, clean ones in the sun. I had
two years to complete my army time. I did it at Fort
Huachuca at the School for the Americas, know as Spy
School. I was in the Urban Warfare section.

"I can't talk about it. It's top secret," I told Nick as
we drove out. "Has to do with the Russkies, the Red
Menace, the Yellow Peril. That's all I am permitted to
say, sir."

We dragged our clothes, boxes of family pictures,
and an old easy chair with an ottoman in an open
trailer behind our Fairlane. We were planning to listen
to country music, drink beer from cans on Saturday
night and get a house with a porch while Nick got himself settled with a good job.

Nick was giddier with every mile that brought us
closer to Sierra Vista. The earth became a new thing as
we drove south out of Tucson. It was like nothing I had
ever seen before or since. The days spent going sixty
miles an hour revealed the cragged, spindly spine of
America. We gawked at it all wordlessly. We felt naive
and insignificant.

34

Driving out of Tombstone at dusk, we pulled over and knelt in the desert. Nick said, "I want to feel this stuff. I just have to feel it."

He gouged at the hard earth and gathered a fistful of dirt. He rubbed the texture, letting it dribble from his hand. We were both afraid to walk more than a few steps into the yawning landscape. The sun threw long shadows as the day rushed toward dark. We weren't scared of scorpions or wild animals. It was because we felt like intruders.

We felt soiled being from Detroit. Detroit, with its clanking factories and shift whistles, its certain work ethic, its hangdog expression at night. In winter, the yellowed city lights pierced the sky and the dirty river creaked on, licking the falling snow into oblivion. That was on a good day.

It was quiet on the side of the Arizona two-lane that night. Someone once said God made the desert so man could find his soul. To us, that night, it was the waiting world, the hard earth. It was a church, and there were rituals it could teach us.

"It's wonderful," Nick said about the dirt in his hand. "It's wonderful."

He scooped up more and washed his hands hard, scrubbing them, twisting them, entwining them, kneading them so the dirt would get in his pores, would become part of his skin. I watched him, and I was scared he was violating a rule.

"What are you doing that for?" I said. "You're getting your hands all dirty. Don't do that, Nick. Come on."

"Try it. It's great. Go on. You'll see."

I looked at the expanse as it slipped into black. I felt shaken and dizzy, alert to my own breathing, aware of the rhythmic feel of blood sliding through my body.

"We should go," I said. "We should go now."

Every moment of that night came back to Nick as he stood and waited to be told I was dead.

"You don't have to lock your doors out here," Nick said the morning after we had knelt in the desert. "People are nice out here. And look at this sky. It's so big. So blue. It was never this big or this blue in Detroit, right? They grow it big out here."

"What kind of blue?" I asked.

"Huh?"

"The sky. How is this blue different from Detroit blue?"

"It's more blue."

He could tell I wasn't buying what he was selling.

"If you had to describe your life as a color, what color would it be?" Nick asked.

"You mean the color it's been up until now?"

"Yeah.

"Gray," I said. "Brown, maybe. Drab. My life's the color of drab."

"Then get ready for blue," Nick said. "Blue, boy. That's the way to go. I'm not talking dark blue. I'm talking sky blue, violet blue, smoke blue—now, that's where the action is. Blue-dress blue. The blues, baby."

Nick had reached over and messed up the little bit of hair that hadn't been buzzed away by a government razor.

"I like green better," I said.

"You'll be green, and I'll be blue," Nick said with a laugh. "Actually, I got it. We can be the Biv Brothers. You can be Roy and I'll be G, and we'll paint the town red every other weekend. What do you say?"

"Green. I like green."

"You're a weird fucking guy, Sam," Nick said to me. "Weird fucking."

Nick snapped out of it when a cop yelled at him to move back from leaning against the police tape. The yellow tape was twirled around wooden sticks then stuck in construction cones all around the Pizza Man for blocks. Just like Perry had expected, they were moving in to categorize everything.

There were two distinct zones now. One was the official zone, with official personnel who patrolled it. The other zone, where Nick was, was civilian. By comparison, it was low-rent. It was just folks, regular people, who had heard what happened and came to see.

They looked at the gathered machinery with awe. They seemed comforted by a helicopter from Fort Huachuca when it landed in the parking lot. They spoke to one another about which kind of terminal event it looked most like. A fire. An explosion. A bomb. 9/11. Oklahoma City. Hostages. Broken water main. A botched robbery.

Nick didn't even consider crossing under the police tape to tell them he was there about me. Nick lived by rules, unlike the two kids near him who darted under the tape and jumped back, thrilled to be part of the scene.

"Excuse me, sir?" Nick said in a whisper to a cop's back. He cleared his throat. "Sir? Excuse me."

The two kids stopped what they were doing. They looked shocked that someone had actually spoken to the policeman. Nick glanced at them and gestured toward the officer, embarrassed he was being ignored.

"He didn't hear me," he said.

"Mr. Police Officer Man," one of the kids yelled. "Oh, Mr. Police Officer, this guy wants you." Then he doubled over laughing.

"Stay behind the tape, boys," the cop said, not turning around until he was done speaking. "Who wants me?"

They pointed at Nick.

"I think my brother might be in there. His name is Sam. I'm looking for him. I got this phone call. From Charlie. Do you know Charlie? He's with the FOP. The Fraternal Order of Police. My brother's name is Sam Tryor."

The cop looked Nick up and down.

"Remain outside the barricades for now. Someone will take your information. In the meantime, I'll have to ask you to please stay on that side of the tape, sir."

"Is he in there? Sam Tryor."

"Someone will be here shortly to speak with you, sir."

"They won't tell me nothing neither," said a young woman. She was pale, wore a halter top and smoked a cigarette like she was attacking it. "That's because they don't know shit. Ain't that right, officer? You don't know shit. Cops. You got a brother in there? My daughter. She works there, and they ain't saying nothing to me. I been here ten minutes, and all they do is tell me not to cross the tape."

The woman radiated the power of someone who spent a lot of time pacing and swearing in small rooms, only going out for cigarettes. Her hair was fastened back from her face. Her body was tough in a small way. She wore fuzzy leopard-print slippers.

"I heard it was a shooting. That's what they said on the TV. Saw it a few minutes ago," said a man in a straw hat. "They say some guy shot the place all up."

"What guy?" a man in a short-sleeved shirt and wide tie asked, moving closer to get in on the impromptu investigation.

"Some nut, probably," the smoking woman said. "Ain't that how it happens? Some asshole goes nuts with an AR-fourteen in a restaurant. Happens every day. Can't turn on the TV without seeing some postal worker or some auto plant asshole shooting twenty people because his hamburger got cooked wrong. Everyone's going postal these days. Unreal."

They all nodded solemnly.

"I heard a gas leak, is all," a young man carrying a motorcycle helmet said.

"But the TV said."

"When's the last time you saw an army Huey—an attack helicopter—at a gas leak? You think they call those things out if it's not serious?"

The man holding his helmet lost his standing.

"They say they're bringing soldiers from the post to help."

"They're bringing cops from Tucson, too."

"That's what we need," the smoking woman said, "more cops. Where were they before this happened? Fucking doughnut shop."

"They can't be everywhere," said a woman with teased hair and over-sized tinted glasses. "If they didn't let everyone walk around with guns this sort of thing wouldn't—"

"If everyone in that place had a gun that guy wouldn't have fired one shot. They woulda shot his ass before anyone got hurt."

"Well…"

"Guns don't kill people," a short, wide man who needed his nose-hairs trimmed said. "People kill people."

"Sure," a young man said, "people with guns."

The conversation lost steam when the helicopter lifted off from the parking lot with its load of wounded. Everyone watched. A few feet off the surface, it looked like an awful miracle. Its blades *thucked* everyone's heartbeat into a shared cadence. Its body hovered like some mythic animal.

As it jolted into the sky, everyone suddenly looked tired of the action. I was grateful when they stopped talking. It was a convention of amateur experts, and it was mean. Where does that come from, I wondered, that casual hate?

I wanted to take Nick away from there. I wished I could have at least gotten him a chair so he could rest.

◦⌒⌒◦

I was with Sarah Tilly as she stood in front of the pay phone outside the Pizza Man. The cell circuits were jammed, and she needed to use that phone. She was trying to gather the guts to call the NBC affiliate in Phoenix.

It was a risky stunt. Cops don't like reporters crawling around fresh crime scenes. And her boss, Jim Smith, wouldn't like it if she tipped off the competition.

This must be done, she thought, dialing the number to the station. I'm not screwing around here. This is television.

"Newsroom," the voice on the phone said.

"This is Sarah Tilly. I need to talk to the news director. Is it still Bob Barlow?"

"That's the guy," the voice said. "He's busy right now. Can I take a message?"

"I need to talk to him. It's about a story."

"You can tell me."

"Listen, pal. I'm standing in the middle of a massacre down here, and I need to talk to Barlow. Interrupt him, put him on the phone, and stop giving me shit."

The girl knew how to hold her ground.

"Hold on," the guy at Channel 8 said. Sarah heard him say, "Bob, some girl on the phone. Says she's at a massacre. That's the actual word she used. She said she wants to talk to you. Then she cursed at me. She said 'shit.' I'll transfer her to your office.

"Hang on," the guy said to Sarah. "I'll transfer you now. And, hey, calm down. All right?"

"Barlow here."

40

She laid it out for him.

"What kind of shooting?" Barlow asked.

"A huge kind," Sarah said. "I was in the restaurant, but they kicked me out."

"Any killed?"

"Some."

"Did you get a count?"

Motherfuck, Sarah thought. A *count*?

"Not yet."

"I thought you said you were inside?"

"I was. They kicked me out."

"What's the address?"

"You can't miss it. It's huge. It's the size of a supermarket. On Fry Boulevard. It's the main drag in town. It's the only drag in town."

"They arrest anyone yet?"

I'm just going to tell this guy what he wants to hear.

"No."

"All right, Sandy, thanks."

"It's Sarah. Sarah Tilly. I sent you a resume two weeks ago. I would love to work for you. I worked at the *Washington Post* and the City News Bureau of Chicago."

"Not ringing a bell. But, thank you."

Sarah played her trump card. There were two things she had; they were the same two things that had the boys opening doors and picking up checks and the girls slamming her down and picking her apart from the time she was twelve years old—lips and hips. Sarah not only had them, she knew how to use them.

"I have long red hair," Sarah said. "I'm five feet, eight inches tall, one hundred-twenty pounds. I'm gorgeous, and I'm a hell of a reporter."

She had just put it all out on the table. Barlow had the next move.

"If you're in the neighborhood tomorrow," Barlow said, "I'll try to make time. No promises."

And he hung up.

Did that just happen? What just happened? Sarah hung up the phone wondering whether she had made a blind date based on phone sex or an appointment for a job interview.

"Jim's been looking for you. Was that him you were talking to?" It was Tom Garrett, the *Herald* photographer. I knew him from somewhere. Where?

She looked at Tom and thought, What a loser. He acts in those plays at the rec center. Probably collects *Star Wars* figurines. I bet he never takes them out of the boxes they came in. He looks like a walking news bureau.

He had three cameras hung around his neck. A bag on his shoulder had two more cameras poking their snouts out. The pockets of his camo-colored vest were stuffed with AA batteries, electronic gadgets, lenses, paper and pens. On a chain he wore a passel of ID tags from the police department, the sheriff's office, Fort Huachuca, the newspaper. Sarah used to kid him that he probably wore his driver's license on a chain around his neck.

I could tell why Sarah didn't see much in him. He looked like he loved playing photographer more than he loved being one.

"Tom," Sarah said. " How'd you get here?"

"I walked. You know, heel-toe, heel-toe. Did you find out what happened?"

"I was inside the place. I'll find Montan."

"Who?" Tom said.

"Lieutenant Montan. The police spokesman? Hello, Tom, are you with me?"

"Would you like to go out sometime?" he said.

Timing, I would have told Tom, is crucial in these matters.

"Now?" Sarah said. "You're asking me this now?"

"Yeah."

"That's sweet, but, no."

Tom didn't say anything. He stood there like he was used to being turned down. Where did I know him from?

"I have to get busy," Sarah said.

"Me, too. I can't believe it. Sam Tryor."

"Sam Tryor what?" Sarah said.

"Don't you know? That's who did it."

She asked how my name was spelled and wrote it down.

"He's a local guy," Tom said, bragging so Sarah might change her mind about a date. "I know him. I don't *know* know him. I've met him."

"Really?"

"He tried out for *Bye Bye Birdie* last summer. Couldn't act worth a damn. I got the lead."

That's where I knew Tom! That prick. I wasn't that bad. I just didn't fit what they were looking for.

"Excuse me." A boy tugged on Sarah's sleeve. He looked young enough to still believe that swallowing gum would do serious bodily damage. "Excuse me."

"What?" Sarah said

"What do the policemen like to eat? They look hungry."

"Well," Sarah said, "doughnuts. Chocolate doughnuts are good."

"'Thanks. I'll get some."

The boy turned and walked away looking straight ahead, thinking about doughnuts.

"You sure you don't want to grab a bite sometime?" Tom said to Sarah.

"I'm seeing someone, Tom," Sarah lied. "But, thanks. That's sweet."

"All right," Tom said, "I'm going to see what I can get. Have fun asking the questions."

The questions. Sarah hated that part of her job. If she had a TV camera, she thought, people would talk to her all damned day. Asking people questions and just writing it down—that was lame. Aside from that, Mrs. Lincoln, how was the play? Tell me, Jesus, did they use sharp or blunt-tipped nails on your feet? It's not cool. It's not close to cool.

I liked Sarah, and not because of her lips or her hips. She was tough, focused and cynical. She wouldn't stop until she found out why I did what I did. Perry and Nick, I realized, wouldn't stop, either. A reporter, a cop and my brother. That was why I was put with those three. My money was on Sarah to get there first.

She set off to do her job...and I was back with Perry.

◦◦◦

He was directing traffic in the restaurant, waiting for the police photographer and the forensics people to come in and start gathering information. Perry told each new paramedic not to touch me.

"He's special," Perry said. "He's not to be moved. He's the shooter. We need him where he is."

He made his detectives stand around so they wouldn't mess up the puzzle pieces of the investigation. The wounded had been removed. The detectives occupied their time among the dead bodies looking at one another, then looking out the window. They examined the blood on the tabletops; they summed up the basic facts and said, in low voices, how terrible, how sick. How could someone? How could someone shoot innocent people while they ate pizza, for God's sakes?

How could I? I wondered. Why would I?

When a new detective came in and made the same comments as the others before, they nodded in grim agreement.

Uniformed police took care of corralling witnesses.

"We simply need to talk to you," they told them. "Then you can go. Do you think you have to go to the hospital? Would you like me to call someone for you? Do you feel up to discussing what happened? Whatever you can remember would help us a great deal."

"Did we get an ID on this nut?" Chief Samson asked Perry. He looked stressed, like he had just rushed in from somewhere he didn't want to leave. He had a bushy white mustache, and he wore round glasses. He had always reminded Perry of someone famous, but he could never place who.

The chief fumbled in his pockets before he settled down to devote his full attention to the matter before him.

"I haven't touched him," Perry said. "I was waiting."

"Good. It's good to wait in these situations. I just had the mayor in my office. The governor called. We don't want this fucked up. We got a lot of dead people here. Lots of media on the way. This has to go right. No fuck-ups, Walter. You got me?"

"Fuck-ups bad. Check."

"I called Homeland Security and the Feds. I called the state forensic guys. They're pros. And Kevin, well..." Samson said about their own forensics man, "this is something a little more complicated than fingerprints at a smash-and-grab."

"Something much more."

"We'll wait for the big dogs and everything will be all right."

The two men thought about the logistics. They worried about what would happen if even one part of the vast, twisted event got out of their control.

"I don't know, Walter," the chief said. "This kind of thing happening here. Jesus. No one is safe. I remember this town when you didn't lock your doors. I mean, no one did. Remember? Shit, if a kid brought a gun to school it would be on the front page for a month. It would be a travesty. Now kids got Glocks, they got Uzis, MAC-tens, all this shit. Little kids, Walter. Maybe it's the home life, I don't know."

They stood in silence for a moment.

"We got at least twenty dead here, Walter," the chief said. "Why? Ralph out there. Poor Ralph, right? Jesus, he's scared. Memorial Day weekend. People. Picnics. The hospital is all full. Helicopters. People screaming."

Perry nodded.

"You want me to ID this guy?" he asked.

The chief put his hand over his mouth and wiped away a slick of sweat. He looked at Perry, trying to tamp down his growing hysteria.

"Yeah," he said. "Go ahead. Why not. Might as well find out."

Perry snapped latex gloves onto his big hands. He carried his own extra-large gloves in his pockets. Protection against who-knew-what. Five-fingered condoms, he thought.

He flexed his hands and knelt next to the sheet. He absently pulled up the wrong end, exposing the head and the face.

My face.

I looked serene. The chief sagged when he saw my face, when he saw the person responsible. He let out a groan then choked it off the second he heard the noise coming from his mouth.

Perry flipped the sheet back over, but it didn't make it all the way. It stopped at my neck and left my face exposed. Perry started to lean over to pull the folded triangle of the sheet straight so I'd be covered, but he got exhausted and stopped. He looked at the white lump of my body under the sheet and thought, You're going to make this tough on me, aren't you? He yanked the sheet completely off me.

I was on my hip, and Perry was thankful, thinking my wallet would be there for the plucking. The wallet, though, was on the side closest to the ground.

"Son of a bitch don't want to give it up," he growled, looking up at the chief. "He's going to give us a time. Oh, yeah. I can tell already."

"Try and not move him too much. We don't want him all moved," the chief said.

Perry carefully turned me so he could get at my pocket. With two fingers, he edged the wallet out. The chief winced. He acted like he and Perry were pickpockets and they could be caught any second now.

Perry straightened up with the prize in his hands. He looked down apologetically.

It's not me, I thought. It's someone who just looks like me. A case of mistaken identity. Maybe I was right in the first place, and I'm here to solve this and clear it up. But who else would wear that tie?

"Let's see," Perry said.

The chief craned his neck, taking care not to move closer to Perry, closer to my body.

"Got a picture here of some guy. There's a credit card, bank card made out to Your Owned Home, Inc. That's out on the highway, isn't it? Some papers, phone numbers. Ah. License."

"Who is he? Please, God, let it be an out-of-towner."

"Nope," Perry said. "Home boy. Samuel F. Tryor. Fifteen-forty East Packer Street. Sierra Vista, Arizona eight-five-seven-nine-two. Organ donor."

"Samuel F. Tryor," the chief said. "Tryor. I know him? You know him?"

"Never heard of him," Perry said.

The wounded and stricken were on their way to hospitals or were outside with paramedics, firefighters, police, and other emergency professionals. Chief Samson and Perry looked around. The place was a mess. Latex gloves, plastic syringe caps, containers, hermetically sealed envelopes for fluids and medicines littered the Mexican tile floor.

I couldn't remember doing it. I tried, but I couldn't. I didn't recall being a "people person," but Jesus, why would I do something like this?

The chief sighed. Perry was thinking that a process had started, that this place was ground zero, a term with the accompanying reverence of being The Place Where the Impact Hits, where the power strikes down and bursts first upon itself before beginning its inevitable outward expansion.

They call the World Trade Center site Ground Zero. This is ours, Perry thought. This room will become enshrined as The Place. It will evoke reverence and moments of silence. There will be a memorial service conducted each anniversary in this big tacky barn with orange walls. The "Southwest's largest pizza palace" is now the Southwest's largest killing field. Down the years, people will tell newcomers about what happened. About the nut. About the shooting, and it was so horrible. And the newcomer will say, "Really? Wow. Why'd the guy do it, they ever find out?"

The owners of the Pizza Man will have to decide whether to reopen the place and when and in what fashion. Who was in charge of clean-up? Will the owners offer some compensation to the customers who were shot or shot at while they ate their pizza?

"They're not saying nothing."

Cortez was in the doorway.

"What?" Perry said.

48

"The victims. We got a bunch of them outside. We were talking to them, you know, getting their names. And they haven't said a word. Hardly."

Perry and the chief didn't say anything.

"We were wondering," Cortez said. "What do we do with them?"

"How many out there?" Chief Samson asked.

"Maybe twenty, twenty-five. There's a bunch more that went to the hospital. Some got flown out. They're real quiet."

Cortez had gotten over the earlier botched dramatics of pulling his gun in front of the Pizza Man. Now he had another crisis to worry about—he had accidentally seen my face and he did not want to see anything else. He didn't want to see the scene in the restaurant. He looked at Perry and the chief for a long time. He looked at them because he did not want to look at the restaurant. If I don't see it, he thought, I won't have to remember it.

"Well, shit, Ralph," the chief said.

Perry thought of Stockholm syndrome, when hostages become close to their taker. It was similar to when people are joined in hard work—together they bring forth the warped and wonderful possibility for true human understanding, even love. Maybe there was some love in this room, Perry thought, startling himself with the word, with the idea.

"Ralph," the chief said, "those poor people just witnessed a slaughter in here." He swept his hand so Cortez could behold. Cortez kept his eyes locked tight to the chief's chin. Don't you follow that man's hand, he thought.

"What the hell do you expect?" the chief said. "This ain't like pulling some guy over for running a red light and having him tell you his life story, now, is it?"

"That's fine," Cortez said. "But what do we do with them?"

"Let me go out," Perry said to the chief. "I'll see what I can see."

Chief Samson followed Perry, who followed Cortez, out of the restaurant.

It was empty except for the dead and me.

It was so quiet. After all the people and the places and thoughts and lives I had visited, there was now only silence. It was peaceful. It was correct. I hoped that soon I would come to know why that was so.

The chief and Perry took deep breaths when they got outside. Cortez walked circles in a daze.

"I know that guy," Cortez said. "Do I? Hold on."

"Hey, Ralph, what's going on?" asked Charlie, the ex-cop who had called my brother and who looked thick and doughy, like Jack Ruby reincarnated.

"He sold my brother his house," Cortez said. "Holy shit. I know that guy."

"What guy are you talking about?" the chief said.

"The shooter. He sold my brother his house."

"Great," the chief said, "the guy's in real estate."

"I remember when he drove us to the trailer park to look at a single-wide," Cortez said. "We just moved here. We were talking about Sierra Vista, about what kind of town it was. He said something."

"What?" the chief said. "What did he say?"

"I'll never forget it. He said, 'Sierra Vista. Military town, sucker town, couldn't give it to me.'"

I went back inside.

Shafts of light came into the restaurant. Through the tinted glass, it looked like an autumn light. The heat from the day still clung to faces, to bare arms and legs. It was like a blanket had been thrown over the entire restaurant.

They were a little more than two hours dead now. It felt like years. Warm and quiet, the bodies were in the same spots they had fallen. It looked like a beach after a battle. Some were arched over booths, some had chair legs on their chests. Many were wrapped around themselves, arms draped over necks and legs and waists, fingers fragile, relaxed and open. They were nonchalant. Some were touching each other, something they would have never done when they were alive. Some corpses were so close together they looked like they were sharing a moment of conversation.

They looked weary but gratified, somehow, relieved and rested after the intense effort they'd made dying. They were waiting for the next stage of activity. The removal and the tags.

Gathering clouds pushed toward the valley from Mexico. Was it a monsoon? Were the late-day rains that come each July early this season? The clouds made the air thick. The atmosphere felt fat, like rain was about to come down.

But there was no payoff yet. The clouds might still bump away harmlessly west, like a big slow-motion pinball ricocheting off the Mule Mountains. Or they would stay, and it would rain tomorrow. That would be good.

The somber scene inside the Pizza Man seemed to have seeped out into the parking lot and the street. It was motionless everywhere. The crowd had shrunk. Things were winding down. The darkening sky had forced a lot of the bystanders away.

Nick stayed. He had told three policemen why he was there, and he was still waiting. He'd been told three times to stay put. Sit tight. Don't move. We'll be back in a few minutes. What's your name again? And what is your brother's name?

He felt foolish standing there. He was in that no-man's land of expectation. He'd waited too long to leave now. He worried it would take a lot longer.

Watching the firefighters sit on the edge of their trucks was getting boring. They weren't speaking to one another. They had been earlier. He looked at the scattered victims, many of whom, for some reason, had blankets around their shoulders. The firefighters had removed their yellow, heavy-gauge emergency clothing. It was in piles around the parking lot, like chunks of mournful confetti awaiting collection.

Nick had stopped looking for my face among the victims.

⁂

Sarah, meanwhile, was trying to get hip-deep in victims.

She spoke to four cops and one ambulance driver after he made a trip back from the hospital. But she wasn't done. She had a list on the cover of her notebook with names of who she had to speak to for her story. Policeman, fireman, medical worker, regular person. She had crossed out each of them and had one left. She needed a victim.

She saw a thick-hipped Hispanic woman who stared at the ground and muttered in Spanish. Not good.

An older man caught her eye. She opened her mouth to speak to him, to rattle off her name and her newspaper. He saw her notebook and waved her off. Then he turned his face away and cried.

Farther on, sitting on the bumper of a police car, was a child. He couldn't have been more than nine. He was watching the firemen and the police.

"Little boy? Little boy?" she said.

He looked at her with his sweet face. He looked fragile and adorable. Sarah thought Tom should take a few shots of him because this is the kid who would make this a real story. Pathetic child. No mommy nearby. Sitting stunned in the carnage. Breaks your heart.

She knelt in front of him.

"Can I ask you some questions? I'm a reporter with the *Herald*. My name is Sarah. What's your name?"

He looked nervous and lost. The blanket was enormous around his shoulders. He had on a baseball cap, backward. His eyes shifted, and his lips tightened.

"What happened in the restaurant? Can I ask you that?" Sarah said. "Can we talk about that?"

The boy looked at her. He inhaled to say something. Sarah put her pen to the paper. The boy lost his train of thought. His looked at his sneakers.

"I bet I can guess your name. It's Larry, isn't it? You look like a Larry."

"No, it's not."

"Jimmy, then."

"You're a reporter? For the paper?"

"Yup, for the *Herald*."

"Can I see your ID? My mom told me not to talk to strangers."

"Sure," she said. She went into her pocket to find her press pass and came up empty. "I have something here, I think. Well, no. I don't have anything with me right now." *Shit. I should wear it around my neck like Tom.* "But I really am a reporter. Really."

Sarah smiled at the boy. Put no sex in it, she thought. Well, maybe a hint.

"Okay," the boy said. "There was this guy, and he had a gun, and he started shooting all over."

The boy looked off and shifted under the blanket.

"Were you scared when he started shooting?"

"Yes."

Sarah wrote "I was real scared" like it was a direct quote.

"It was lots of noise in there."

He's opening up, Sarah thought. This is going to work out. She looked up at him, imploring him to, please, continue.

"People were getting hurt."

"Were your mommy or daddy in there with you?"

"They were there with me."

Kid sees Mom and Dad cut down.

"And they're not now?"

"I don't know where they are. It was a lot of shooting."

"Did you see the man? Do you know what he looked like?"

"I didn't see him real good. I don't remember. He had a gun, though. A big one."

"All right," Sarah said, flipping a page filled with scribbled notes that she, through some miracle, would be able to decipher later. "Was he a big man? A short man? Did he say anything?"

The child kicked his feet and bounced his heels off the ground. Sarah waited for delivery of the goods.

The boy looked her up and down and said, "Is this off the record or on?"

A third-grader going on background? Unfuckingreal.

"This is on," Sarah said. "I'm going to use this in the article."

"No," the boy said, shaking his head. "I don't want to be in the paper. I don't think it would be right."

"It's okay. It's no big deal. This is how it works. You talk to me, I write it down then I put it in the paper. You want to be in the paper?"

"I got to go now."

"What's your name?"

"Bye."

I can still use it, Sarah thought. She wrote down a quick description of the kid. She added details. She wrote that he wore Nike sneakers, had a green blanket around his shoulders, he wore a T-shirt with the words "NO FEAR" in fuscia and chartreuse. She wrote that his name was Jimmy.

〜〜

The pressure from the clouds gave Perry a sinus headache. He stood in the parking lot, pinched his nose to get a little relief, and looked at the sky.

Samuel F. Tryor. Organ donor, he thought. Will anyone want his organs? Do the recipients know who it comes from? A heart. A liver. An eye. Can they refuse if they know? Would they? Would I? Are they told?

He looked at the police. They were tired from standing around for so long. He knew they needed assignments before they had the chance to think too much.

Most cops, Perry thought, are better off not thinking most of the time. There is a lack of form in this place. We are lacking protocol and purpose.

"Bill," he said to one he recognized.

"Name's Dave."

"Dave. The guy who did the shooting? His name's Tryor. Try and find a relative. The whole damned town is here. Maybe he's got someone. But be cool about it. Okay?"

"Sure. I'll take Ralph along. Fucking mess, huh?"

"Tryor. T-R-Y-O-R. Got it?"

Perry savored the calm. The satellite trucks and the other police agencies and the whole world hadn't shown up yet. He tried to make the shooting exist only as the repetition of bullets and facts, figures, angles, trajectories. He went down a checklist of tasks. It was as simple to him as it had been in kindergarten when the to-do list was tying shoes, working buttons and napping. On the top of his list was crime scene preservation.

I pictured a large vat of thick liquid into which the crime scene was submerged.

Next was categorizing the evidence, collecting statements, comparing divergent versions of the crime, contacting and briefing cooperating agencies. In his thoughts, he used those terms—*crime scene* and *cooperating agencies*—because he found comfort in police-speak neutrality. The intoxicated perpetrator was apprehended. Exit wound. Code-4. Proceeding at a high rate of speed. Victim assault. The emotionless language warped reality. It helped his mind function better.

Samuel F. Tryor 1540 East Packer Street, Sierra Vista, Arizona 85792. I wonder what the F. stands for.

It stood for Francis, my father's name.

◦◦◦

"Ma'am? Do you know a man named Tryor?" Officer Dave asked a woman.

"My brother, he in there."

"Yes, ma'am. Was his name Tryor? T-R-Y-O-R?" Cortez asked her.

"Gamez. Rudolfo Gamez," the woman said, crying.

The two policemen moved on, although they first cast their eyes down to acknowledge the poor woman's loss.

I can't stay here forever, Nick thought. What am I even thinking? Sam's probably home worrying I'm in there dead.

He didn't move, though. He stayed stuck to that spot. He stayed because it was a chance to do something. He wanted answers, and he wouldn't get them bouncing off the walls at home.

"These people," Cortez said to Dave.

"Yeah," Dave said. "Like lawyers at a bus crash."

"These people."

"Like insurance adjusters after a hurricane."

They split up to search for someone who would look like their name was Tryor.

Cortez was impressed with himself, especially with the way he'd survived the trauma of the original call. He was first on the scene. He'd drawn his gun for the first time in his career. That was some dangerous action. Now he was at point, in charge, as it were, of bagging the prime suspect. As it were.

That's when he found Nick.

"Mr. Tryor, would you wait right here for a moment," Cortez said in a tone that made it clear it was not a request. He was shocked that he'd found the mythical "Tryor." He went off to find help, unsure whether he should cuff, comfort or confront the guy.

He didn't say "Please," Nick thought. Does that mean something? I did something wrong. Something is not right. The police don't tell you not to move at a place where people were gunned down for no reason. Is Sam all right?

Soon, they would tell him what I did. For the first time since I died, I was afraid—afraid for Nick.

He lit a cigarette. The boy with the box of doughnuts was staring at him.

It's like, Nick thought, slowing down when you see a police car, even though you weren't speeding. You see the officer's head swivel in your direction. You're separated from the herd, and you believe cops can read minds or there was a thing you did that was bad, very bad, so you flip through your brain trying to get your fingers around the thing you did, going back to Original Sin, so you can develop an explanation, get your ducks in a row...only you're too stupid to know what it is and now they're on you. Fuck.

"See?" Cortez said to Dave, pulling him toward Nick.

"See what?"

"I didn't ask him to wait. You can't ask people sometimes. Sometimes you just have to tell them. This was one of those times."

"Wow, Ralph, you are some kind of a cop's cop."

"Today, yes, I am."

The kid with the doughnuts gripped his box. He stared at Nick. He put the heat on him because Nick was having some dealing with the police.

Nick shrugged and smiled. But the kid bored it in and poured it on. The heat.

"My brother," Nick said to the kid. "I think he was in there. They probably need to talk to me all about it, just to make sure he's okay."

The kid didn't say a word.

"Could I have a doughnut?" Nick asked.

"They're only for police officers. They like doughnuts."

"I like doughnuts, too."

"You're not a police."

I am cut from the herd. I am outside society. I am an "other."

"You got that right," Nick said. "Cops do like their doughnuts."

"What did you do?" the kid asked.

"Nothing. I told you, I think my brother was in there."

"You must've done something if the police want to talk to you."

Nick knelt until he was at eye-level with the kid. He saw Cortez and Dave coming his way.

"I'll tell you what I done, kid, if you give me them doughnuts."

The kid clasped the doughnut box tighter, but he was considering the deal.

"Better hurry," Nick said. "They're coming. They're coming to get me."

The kid handed over the box like he was handing over his ticket to the biggest ride at the carnival.

Nick stood up, looked down at the kid and said. "You know what I did?"

"What?"

"I stole a little boy's doughnuts."

Way to go, Nicky. Way to go.

"Mr. Tryor," Cortez said. "Please come with us."

"You boys want a doughnut?" Nick said.

He opened the box, and it was empty.

Way to go kid. Way to go.

〰️

A moment later, Sarah got busted.

"Did you get everything you need, Sarah?"

She stopped cold. She knew Lt. Montan's voice.

"You have to leave, Sarah," he said. "You've had your fun, now play by the rules."

"Tell me how many dead. I need a number."

"We'll have a press availability later, at the station," he said, pushing her toward the edge of the parking lot. "You'll get everything you need then."

"Come on, Steve. Look, I'll be at your press thing. I'll be in the first row. I just need to get an idea of what we're dealing with before then. I've heard as many as twenty dead. Is that fact or fiction?"

"That's math."

"*Steve.*"

"I've had seventeen voice mails in the last fifteen minutes. I got television stations headed here from as far away as California. I can't play favorites with you today. They're coming, and they're headed straight for me. I bet if you put your hand to the ground you can feel the vibrations of their trucks and their blow-dryers. Give it a rest and step back behind the tape."

Montan held the tape line up over Sarah's head. She took her place on the other side of the tape with all the other civilians.

It was a setback, but my money was still on her.

"Jim wants us back," Tom said, coming out of nowhere. "He's wondering why he hasn't heard from you yet."

"I've been busy."

"Doing what?"

"Baking cakes."

"You better whip up something good because Jim wants to put out an extra edition of the paper. Today."

I stood with Perry and Chief Samson. We watched the state police and Homeland Security and the FBI arrive. They unloaded their gear without a word. They wore hard faces and crisp uniforms. Chief Samson thought they had amazing equipment.

"Those guys are always taller than our guys," he said.

"Better funding," Perry said.

"Pisses me off, their height."

"We got the shooter's brother in a car," Perry said to the chief. "Should we talk to him or give him over to them?"

"Give him over after we talk to him. You do it. Find out what you can. Maybe we can put all this to rest today. Could be the guy had a tumor in his brain. That would be great. A mass as big as a grapefruit."

"Tumors are always compared to fruit. Why is that?"

"Don't know."

"Maybe cancer," Perry said. "Could be AIDS. A touch of the AIDS."

"Just a touch."

"Five months to live. I could see that."

"That guy in the tower in Texas? He have a tumor?"

"I think he was a Satan worshiper. Pentagrams and killing goats."

"That was Son of Sam. Berkowitz."

"Sam the dog," Perry said. "Told him to do it."

"Then the Texas guy, he must have had a tumor."

"Zodiac. That was a Satan guy."

"Yup."

"John Wayne Gacey. What was his deal?"

"Same as Dahmer," Chief Samson said. "Sick fag. Sat on Nancy Reagan's lap, didn't he?"

"I think that was Bundy."

"They fried him."

I knew they were only talking tough because that was a way people dealt with terrible situations. But still, I hadn't been dead more than a couple of hours, and I was being mentioned in the same breath as Ted Bundy. As Jeffrey Dahmer. As John Wayne Gacey. At this rate, by tomorrow, I'd be right up there with Hitler.

"I wonder what our boy's problem was," the chief said.

"Homosexual dog-owning devil worshiper with a brain growth and two months to live," Perry said.

"One can only hope."

Nick didn't talk when they walked him to the police car. He thought about his last run-in with the cops. Even then, it was my fault.

Nick and I were kids hunting crayfish in a pond on Belle Isle outside Detroit. We had rolled up our pants and were tramping around in the mush of the pond bed catching and putting the crayfish in a plastic bucket. Some older kids told us we would get arrested for being in the pond.

"Read the sign—no swimming," they said.

Nick wanted to take the crayfish home and raise them. I told him they weren't like pets.

"You can't train them or anything," I said.

But he kept on collecting. He picked them up, placed them carefully in the bucket, added water to the bucket, asked about what they ate, and wondered where we could find them food.

"Look at that big one," Nick said. "He's real big. I want to name him Craig."

We were such doofus kids.

"Mr. Tryor, we're taking you to the station," Cortez said to Nick. "If you want to call a lawyer, you can do that."

"Watch your head here, Mr. Tryor."

"We could get in big trouble for this," I'd told Nick. "If you see any cops, jump out and I'll handle it."

He kept on collecting, and sure enough, a few minutes later, two park rangers showed up in a little boat.

"Come on up out of there," one said. "Didn't you see the sign? Can't you read? I think what we got here is a couple of dummies who can't even read."

"Careful, here, Mr. Tryor," Cortez said. There were people closing in on the police car.

The kids who had warned us about the crayfish kept staring at us while I gave the park rangers our address and names. Nick kept the bucket with the crayfish on his lap and let me handle the cops.

I was so embarrassed. Nick didn't say anything when the park rangers dumped the crayfish back into the pond. He didn't say a word when we were followed home and called stupid jerks by the kids.

We got youth delinquent warnings. Fat envelopes of legal-looking paperwork showed up at the house a week later. Our father thought it was hysterical. He called us "desperado delinquents." Our mother gave us a stern look. And that was our big brush with the law until Nick was placed in the back of Cortez's cruiser.

When the car door was slammed, Nick said, "There are no handles on these doors."

The clouds were closing in on the town. The first of the satellite news trucks turned off the highway and headed to the scene.

— 6 —

In 1863, a ghost led an eleven-year-old child to the murder site of a Catholic priest in Bethesda, Maryland. The priest had been battered over the head with a shovel and put in a grave dug for someone else.

The child led police to the site and said he had been taken there by the murderer. He said the man was so guilt-stricken he'd committed suicide, but he couldn't rest until he told someone what he had done. That's why he'd come to the child—to make amends.

The grave the child led them to, it turned out, was intended for his father, and the priest that very day had presided over the burial.

The child was sent to an asylum for the criminally insane, where he died sixty years later. He was buried next to his father, and went to his grave having never once changed his story that a ghost came to him to confess and make amends.

❦

I was in Veteran's Park, across from the Pizza Man. It was a beautiful evening. It was that slate-sky time of day, warm, normal and soothing, especially away from the lights and the blood.

A woman stood in the parking lot looking madder than hell.

I thought I had broken the code and was linked to Perry, Sarah and Nick to find out why I did what I did. Now what? It would have been nice to have had a Jacob Marley who could have run down the rules at the start of the game for me. I didn't know why I was in that park, but I figured that, unlike in *A Christmas Carol*, it wasn't to learn the true meaning of Christmas.

Several men strolled around in the park with their late-day cans of beer. A band in lederhosen and American Legion poppies played listlessly. The sad sounds joined the voices of the scattershot crowd.

This was Sierra Vista. It was 40,000 people, a Walmart, a mall and an army post. It was fast food places, trailer parks and Arizona sprawl. It was home.

"Let the kid be, Phyl," the angry woman's husband said. "Come on. It's a holiday here. We're having us a holiday."

Phyl shrugged him off and glared at the kid, who was getting closer to her. He looked at the ground and walked that penitent walk.

It was the kid with the balloon. I had wanted to be with him, and there I was. Perhaps I was gaining some control over my ghostly powers and might have something to move from the Bad side of the list to the Good. He was same kid who'd had the doughnuts.

"What did I tell you?" Phyl said to her son.

The child said nothing. He looked over at the remaining emergency lights swirling across the street.

"Get your things," Phyl said. "We're leaving. Help your father load the car."

"Can I go over to the ducks real quick?"

"We don't need no ducks."

"Let him go over real quick," the father said. "They're just ducks, for Christ's sake."

"Make it quick," she said, outnumbered and now really pissed off.

❦

The scene in the park was winding down. I remembered that it was Memorial Day. Anyone who couldn't afford to get out of town had stopped by the park to hear the mayor say remember the dead, hear the DARE officer tell everyone to say no to drugs, hear Ms. Mountain View say whatever it was she had to say.

The kid went to the duck stand. It felt nice and cool under the tent because of the running water from the game. I used to play this same game. For fifty cents, they gave you a net, the kind you use to scoop fish from an aquarium. Yellow hard-plastic ducks raced along on the current on an oval track of water and you had to snag a duck to win a prize.

"Everyone's a winner here. Scoop a duck, win a prize," the guy manning the booth said.

Some ducks had red dots underneath. If you got one of those, you won the big prize—a real, live baby duck. There were twenty ducklings nestling in the center of the tent. They were surrounded by chicken wire, like if they weren't caged they'd get out and viciously attack people. Anything other than a red dot would only get you something lame, like a plastic bubble pipe or a toy car.

The kid was hellbent on a duck. He watched the plastic ducks going around, biding his time to select the one.

"Mister?" the kid said. "I got fifty cents. Can I go? I'll make it real quick. I won't ask to go again if I lose. Promise."

He'd been there a few times before and only come away with Matchbox cars, all Novas.

"All right," the guy said. "But make it fast. I want to get the hell out of here while I'm still young."

The kid gripped the net. He zeroed in on his duck as it went around. The entire world to him was that piece of molded yellow plastic. He squared his shoulders. He was ready to thrust the net out and snag his duck.

"You put that down!"

It wasn't his mother. It was some other lady, but she was mad, too.

"I want to talk with you," the woman said to the kid. "Do you know where those ducks come from? Disgusting. Do you know what happens to them? You have no idea. I said put that down."

"What do you mean 'Put it down?'" the guy running the stand said. "Don't you put nothing down, kid. Hang tight for a minute, little brother."

The woman stood behind the kid at the duck stand. She held his shoulders.

"These ducks get killed by children," the woman said. "They get them, and they torture them and kill them. You don't care. As long as you get your fifty cents, it's all fine by you."

The kid was stuck between the two arguing adults. He was trying desperately to concentrate on his plastic duck. He was tracking it, but it was tough to keep an eye on it with these two getting in his way.

"Lady, let the kid play the game. He's the last one. Let him play, then I can go home and you can go save the spotted owl and everybody will be happy."

"Listen," the woman said. "You're a good person. I know you are. You want to help. I know you do. Just give me the ducks. I'll make sure they're okay."

"You're going to make sure?"

"Yes. I'll find them homes. Good homes where they won't get pelted to death with rocks by some little… little bastard kids all mad because they won't quack. Come on, what do you say?"

"Lady, for all I know you're in the paté business," the guy said. "Now get out of here before I call a cop on your ass. Pick your duck, kid. Let's go."

"You can't do this, "the woman said. "Put the net down."

"You got two seconds, kid."

"Don't do it."

I had forgotten how tough kids have it. They're always stuck between opposing forces telling them what they should do.

The kid was tired of being in the middle. He thrust the net in and snagged his duck. He shut his eyes and handed it to the guy behind the counter. The lady stared at him with her hot, animal-loving eyes. I was thrilled for the kid's act of rebellion. He didn't know what or who he was rebelling against, but it felt good to see.

The kid turned the duck over. No red dot. Damn. The kid heard his mother's voice in the distance. He had to go.

"All right! Kid! You're a winner," the guy running the stand said. "This is great. You want a duck? Take a duck."

The guy bent over the chicken wire, all the time smirking at the animal-rights woman, and scooped up a small, barely feathered trembling creature. His stare never left the woman as he gave the duck to the kid.

The woman made a glancing move to get the duck. The kid was having none of it. He held it close to his chest and shot her a look that would have frozen fire.

"He's putting the moves on you, lady," the guy said. "I don't think he's going to give him up."

"Who's in charge here?" the woman said. "I'll talk to them about what's going on here. I'll straighten this out."

She looked around at the closing, worn-out carnival for someone official to hear her out. But anyone in

— *Alex O'Meara*

charge of anything was across the street dealing with bigger matters.

"Don't you move," she said. "Either of you. I will be right back."

"Thanks, mister," the kid said. "What does this duck eat? I got to get him—"

"Get the fuck out of here, kid. I got things to do."

⁂

The child tucked the duck under his shirt. He smoothed it down and told the duck his name was Simon. He tried to act natural when he saw his mother. He felt like he'd been gone for a year.

"Where you been?" Phyl said. "Didn't you hear me calling for you? Tell me you didn't hear me?"

"I didn't hear you."

She slapped him. She was not the kind of woman to lose a battle of wits with an eight-year-old twice in one day. His rebellion was over.

Her husband, sitting with both hands on the steering wheel, concentrated exclusively on the dashboard.

"Get in the car," Phyl said.

The child didn't cry. He squared his shoulders, took a step toward the car…and stopped cold when the duck landed at his feet.

"What's that?" his mother said. "What is that?"

The father tucked his chin down to his chest and tightened his grip on the steering wheel.

"Nothing."

"Nothing? Doesn't look like nothing. Does it look like nothing to you?"

"No."

"Get in the car."

"But…"

"Tell me you didn't hear that. Tell me you didn't hear me just tell you 'Get in the car.'"

The child didn't bite. It was a fix. He'd get hit.

70

Phyl picked up the duck in one hand and pointed at the stand with the other.

"Is that where it came from?" she asked the kid, who was now sitting in the back seat of the car.

"The man give it to me. His name's Simon."

"Well, now, Simon can take it back."

"*His* name's not Simon. The duck's name is Simon."

I stayed with the kid as he watched his mother walk to the duck stand. She and the guy who ran it spoke. The kid could tell they were mad at each other. Anyone could tell that. The guy at the stand shook his head as Phyl held the duck out to him.

He won't take it back, the kid thought. He ain't going to take Simon back. So, now we got to keep him.

He saw his mother weigh the duck in her hand like it was a rock she was going to throw. Then she looked around.

The kid sat up in the back seat and looked straight ahead. He smiled. He'd won.

Good for you, kid, I thought. Good for you.

His mother got in the car and said, "Let's get going."

"Are you going to give him his duck so we don't have to hear about it all the way home?" her husband asked.

"The duck's taken care of. Let's go."

"What did you do with it, Phyl? You didn't..."

"Drive."

The kid looked out the back window. He hoped to see that woman from before. He looked all over for that woman. *Where is that woman?*

He didn't see her. He looked for Simon, but he couldn't see the duck anywhere on the ground. He looked. He looked hard. He saw piles of popcorn on the grass. He saw some trash that would never be picked up. He saw the guy from the duck stand all packed up. He noticed a crowd of people on the sidewalk just outside the park entrance. Some of them were pointing across the street at the Pizza Man. He saw all the crazy red and blue emergency lights in the parking lot.

The kid didn't notice the green oil barrels filled with garbage. They never registered on him, and the duck was never mentioned again.

What happened to that kid was worse than anything I'd seen that day. A million times worse. I thought if I had a gun right then I would have used it on the kid's mother. And I wouldn't have spared his mope of a father, either.

—7—

Where did I get the guns? How many guns did I use? Why did I do it?

Perry was close to my body. It was at his feet. I had so many questions. He had more. How many were dead?

I marveled at the efficiency of the men in the Pizza Man as they removed the bodies. It was dark, and they used flashlights instead of putting the lights on so people couldn't look in at them while they worked. I had never seen this sort of thing done on television or read about it in the newspaper. I never met anyone at a party who talked about doing this kind of work. If I had, I wouldn't have talked to them for long. It wasn't sexy or interesting. It was completed then forgotten, even by those who did it, I imagined.

It reminded me of moving day, when you stand off to the side and watch a bunch of guys handle your most precious possessions. All your stuff is hoisted up into arms and on backs. You feel like a fool if you help, more foolish if you don't. *Be careful with that. It's fragile.*

"No, not him. He goes last," Perry said to a paramedic who came to get me.

73

That box will go in the dining room. It's got china in it. All of China.

There was barely a sound except for Perry telling the men not to move me.

"We're waiting on this one," he said, and they moved on silently.

One, two, three, five, nine unzipped bags were laid out. One body at a time was moved on top of each flattened bag. Then the black plastic sack was stretched out on the sides and the zipper was pulled to seal the cargo. One rubber-gloved paramedic nodded to the other and then all three—do you count them as three if one's dead?—moved out. Then again. And again. And again.

Did I have an accomplice? Did I plan it like I was some survivalist nut holed up in a dank basement plotting to assassinate a visiting dignitary?

I lost count of the bodies and started estimating. Twenty. Thirty. Did I count them when I shot them? Was I trying to achieve a certain number?

The men didn't say a word when they shifted the weight over onto the body bag, wrapped the sides, zipped it shut, picked it up and lugged it out. The bags looked like sacks of dripping-wet grain, the kind they had on a farm after a flood.

Perry thought the zipping sounded like a fishing reel that was cast, got snagged and stopped.

When they were outside, did the paramedics speak to one another? "Boy, this is a fat one, huh?" "Look at those hooters!" What, exactly, was considered bad taste in a distasteful line of work? Were they taught how to do this so silently in a school? Was there a class on how to signal to one another using nods, eye gestures and hand movements, like a baseball manager or a deaf person who speaks with those finger gymnastics?

There were two left. Women. One blond, the other brunette. Two women and me.

Perry looked down at me. Look at you, he thought. What do you know? Everything. You know it all. The reason. Or reasons. And we're all going to run around trying to figure out why you did it. And you're going to just lay there knowing.

All the work we'll go through. The chalk line drawings. The diagramming. Reconstructing last moments. Counting bullets. Do the number of wounds and misses equal the number of bullets in the clips? Impact. Trajectory. Numbers. Firing patterns. Witness statements. Photos. Blood smears. What were you thinking, Sam F. Tryor, when you did it?

Was it, I wondered, a mission that involved the CIA or the army, like a Manchurian Candidate sort of thing? Was there a grand and sweeping story behind my pathetic, nasty act? Was there a possibility I wasn't guilty? I thought about my own life and everything I didn't know about it. I thought about how much effort goes into a single life.

These poor people. They were dead, but they went to school, they learned, they had their hopes and dreams. They watched television and saved their money for that vacation. Their parents worried they would be hit by a car crossing the street. But, Mom… Wear your mittens, it's cold out. But, Mom…

Did my parents worry about me like that? Or did they make jokes about how I was a moody kid, the type who would grow up and go to the top of a tall building with a high-powered rifle one day?

"Lieutenant, that's it on those," one of the paramedics said to Perry. "We can take your guy now."

"Okay," Perry said distractedly.

The paramedics stood in front of him.

"Yes?" he said to them.

"Little space here, sir? That's it. Make a hole. Thanks."

He moved to accommodate them.

My body bag was rolled out, curling on the ends like a section of black sod to be tramped down. They must have been glad their work was almost over. I was the last. One stood at my shoulders, his partner at my feet. They counted.

"On three. Ready. One, two, thr—"

"Wait. Hold it up," one of the paramedics said.

"What? What's the trouble?"

The two men straightened up and looked down. They consulted. There was a problem with me.

"His head," the first one said. "That's a pretty big hole. We have to plug it, if we want him to keep his brains."

"Get a trauma pad," the other paramedic said. "We'll tape him up."

While they waited, Perry and the paramedic looked everywhere but at one another, the way people do in elevators.

"Big mess, huh?" the paramedic said.

"Yeah," Perry said. "Big."

"I ain't never seen this many bodies in one place before. Don't know where we're going to put them all. Morgue's full. They got them down the halls over there. Unreal."

"Yeah."

"I hope we have a trauma pad left. If not we'll have to rig something. But, don't worry. We'll make it so he, you know, so he keeps his brains."

"Yeah."

"Though, I guess he wouldn't be the first one to lose his brains here today."

"What?" Perry asked.

"Nothing."

"Got it," said the first paramedic, who came back with a huge swatch of gauze. "Last one, too."

The two men bent down, slipped the pad under my head and taped it to my skull. I looked ridiculous.

"That'll hold."

"Good deal. On three. One, two, three."

❦

Perry walked alongside the men as they carried me. Were we three people or four? Or were we five? Did my ghost count as a person?

To Perry, it felt like days had gone by since he pulled up and kept Ralph from shooting that guy. He was weary; the weight of the day pressed upon him.

He saw a satellite news truck and felt like he should go over and, all cop-like, tell them, *Move it, buddy. This is a crime scene, here.* But he didn't. Who cares, he thought. They'll ask me questions. They'll broadcast whatever I say. "Exclusive!!" no matter what I say.

There was still a crowd, but they were different. They looked like they were there only because they had nowhere else to go.

My body was loaded into an ambulance. They threw me, on the count, after three swings, on top of the pile.

"If that's it, Lieutenant, we're out of here."

"Where's this one going?"

"They got a room set up at the hospital for the overflow."

"No good. That last guy, take him to the morgue."

"There isn't room."

"Make room. Move someone. I don't care what you do. Understand? And I want him in a cooler or a drawer and not spoiling in some hall. I also want an MRI of his head and I want someone to pull his medical records. Tonight. I'll be along to check."

They were serious about looking for a tumor in my brain. A big growth pressing on my amygdala would get me and everyone else off the hook. Then why did I want a gun back in the Memorial Park? Did my ghost have a brain tumor? I doubted it.

The ambulance left. Perry watched it go, then turned and went to his car.

I wondered why they took dead people away in ambulances. Do they bother to run the sirens, or is it always just the lights?

Perry radioed in. He was told Nick was in the chief's office waiting to be interviewed.

"I'll be there shortly," he said. "Try and free a real room, not the chief's office. And, yes, I know the state guys are looking for me. The Homeland Security guys. The FBI guys. Tell them I'll get with them as soon as I can."

Wild animals know to rest on the move, Perry thought. They relax between efforts. They ride waves of exertion. A leopard in the Serengeti never had to solve a mass murder, though. There wasn't a single one that ever had the Feds breathing down his neck for answers.

Perry stood at his car and took a look around. What's going to happen here has happened, he thought. We know what happened. We know where it happened. The experts will move in to evaluate. Bits of information will go into glycine envelopes. Pieces will be labeled, filed, dug out, examined and fitted. They'll tell us precisely what happened. Weapons have been recovered. Good. The main thing is to not overreach. We must not make anything up. We must not jump to any conclusions.

Perry pulled his car out onto Fry Boulevard. He joined a long line of cars going slowly past the Pizza Man. People craned their necks to see the place where it happened. They bowed their heads in acknowledgment, sighed, then checked themselves out in their rearview mirrors, switched radio stations, exchanged looks and shared a shake of the head about what the world was coming to. One beautiful black-haired woman concentrated on something and sat with her forefinger deep in her nose.

A few blocks later, Perry's mind loosened when the traffic started to move again. As if wiping sleep away while driving a long distance, he shook his head and renewed his effort to get down to the heart of his investigation:

Man walks into a restaurant and kills forty people. Then he shoots himself. He was in a bad mood? He didn't like his pizza? His wife recently left him? He got fired from his job? Is he a member of a militia making a point about how fast food saps the stability of national security? Is he plain old nuts? Did he mean to only shoot the man who plowed into his car in a supermarket parking lot then took off saying nothing, but he got carried away? *Do not get ahead of yourself. Concentrate on the facts alone and follow them.*

The count was forty. I had killed forty people.

Perry saw a small red-and-white square bumper sticker on a Honda Accord. It said: MEAN PEOPLE SUCK. The car stopped short in front of Perry, and he almost rammed it.

"Hey," he barked. "Don't be an asshole. Let's go, you mean person who sucks."

Perry reviewed the known facts:

White male, aged fifty-two years old from Sierra Vista, armed with a semi-automatic weapon and a handgun, opens fire at about three p.m. No reports—thus far—from any witnesses that the man demanded, wanted or desired anything. No indication of accomplices. No signs of robbery or theft. Man is not known to local authorities. *No, wait. We don't know that for sure.* Man shoots self with pistol. Event ends. Got it. The who, what, where, how and when. Sealed. What about the why?

Why?

There it was. I had shot myself. I was raised Catholic, and I had committed the ultimate sin. Now I knew everything except the answer to the same question Perry was asking.

Why?

There is a silence that can come to you when the biggest question remains, when you realize that everything you know is not enough. It can come when you realize you may never know enough.

Alone, in the middle of that silence, Perry missed the turn into the police station and had to circle the block.

— 8 —

On August 27, 1977, in Austin, Texas, John Small was killed after the brakes on his truck failed while he was hauling a load of tires to the dump. Small owned a trucking company with his brother-in-law, Bill Rinehart. A picture of Rinehart and Small at a ribbon-cutting ceremony marking the expansion of their company appeared on the front of the business page of the *Austin American Statesman*—five years after Small died.

You can see where this is going. Rinehart was all smiles in the photo, but Small didn't look too happy. In fact, he looked five years dead and extremely angry. A few days after the picture appeared in the *Statesman*, Rinehart broke down and confessed he had cut the brake lines on Small's truck.

Jules Linton has haunted the *Cleveland Plain Dealer* newspaper since October 15, 1927. That was his last day as managing editor, the day he "fell" into the presses and was, literally, pressed to death. Every October 15, Linton's obituary ends up on the *Plain Dealer*'s presses when they're ready to roll.

Dead people liked to use the media to tell their stories. I was different. When I found myself in a news-room, I hoped the media would help *me* learn my story.

◦◦◦

Jim Smith, Sarah's editor, was glad Sarah was on the story. She was good. He thought that, despite her mistakes, despite that she'd called Channel 8 and tipped them off, and her history of making up quotes, she had real street smarts.

Although he had called in Tom and the other reporters—Fred and Stan, like a pair in silent movies who paint houses badly, and Barbara Cloven, a squat woman Sarah called The Hoof—he was counting on Sarah.

He recalled when he'd first met her. Her interview had been so promising. Sitting in his office, he'd smiled at her and said, "I hear you're a regular fuck-up, Miss Tilly."

◦◦◦

She smiled back at him, a gorgeous, radiant smile.

"Don in DC tells me you're screwing up. He tells me you've been making up quotes. You're making up whole stories. He says you should be in the *AP Stylebook* under F, for fuck-up."

I wonder if she can tell I rehearsed this speech? Smith thought.

"Don also tells me you're a real hotshot, leave-the-money-on-the-bed kind of girl. But he also says you're a good reporter. I owe Don a favor, so I said I would take you on. The ground rules are, I don't want anyone misquoted." He stopped pacing and glared at her. Then he slammed his knee into his desk. "Shit," he said. I didn't rehearse that, he thought. "Where was I?"

"'Under F in the *Stylebook*,'" Sarah said. "'Don't want anyone misquoted.'"

"I don't want you to make anything up, like in Washington. I don't want this paper hurt in any way. That happens, and I cut you loose."

"Is that all?"

"Yup."

"Thank you for the opportunity," Sarah said. "I'll make the most of it."

"I know you will. You'll cover general assignments and cops. Welcome to the Sierra Vista *Herald.*"

⌒〜⦾

Sarah did make the most of it. She'd seemed happy. What happened?

Two weeks before the shooting, she had decided on a new and higher calling, one in which her looks would make her a treasure instead of a drool-soaked fantasy. She turned to embrace the holy, apostolic religion of television. At least, that's what Jim's buddy at Channel 8 told him.

She'll get over it, he thought, chalking it up to her age.

He relaxed and enjoyed the weight of his own importance as a newspaper editor in a small town when a huge thing happens. He sat at his desk with his palms facing one another. He did the old "Here's the church, here's the steeple. Open the door, see all the people," but he added "shot dead like dogs," and caught himself smiling. Then he rubbed his hands together, went to make coffee, and waited for the action to start rolling.

⌒〜⦾

"I got the best stuff out there," Sarah said when she came in. "This one kid was great."

"Where the fuck have you been?"

"Covering the story," she said, backing into a chair. "I was covering the story."

"I need whatever you have ten minutes ago. Nothing fancy. We're doing an extra, so make it fast. I don't care about pretty."

She sat down to write, and a few minutes later, Jim showed up again and hovered over her.

"You're making it hard for me to concentrate."

"I'm the editor. I get to do what I want."

"Go away, Jim."

He left.

It was time to see how Sarah would tell my story, time to get some answers.

She wrote:

> A crazed gunman opened fire today in a crowded restaurant. At least 20 innocent men, women and children were cut down in a hale of bullets.
>
> Police this afternoon are picking through the blood-soaked result of the rampage.
>
> Some whacko nut job went berserk today with a high-powered elephant gun, and for some stupid reason murdered till he could not murder no mo', no mo', and then did the honorable thing and sucked the pipe, police say.

Sarah looked at Smith in his office. She wanted to taunt him like you tease a ferocious animal safely behind bars at the zoo. She wanted to plant her thumbs on the sides of her head and wave her hands while sticking out her tongue. Instead, she got back to it and wrote:

> At least 20 and as many as 40 people were killed at the Pizza Man restaurant earlier today by a lone gunman who took his own life.
>
> "It was real scary," said a nine-year-old boy in a T-shirt that read "NO FEAR," who apparently was in the restaurant when the shooting started. "I

wasn't really scared. Well, yeah, I was. And all the people…"

State and local police, sheriff's deputies, and soldiers from Fort Huachuca, along with emergency personnel from as far away as Tucson, responded to treat the wounded. Sierra Vista Community Hospital was overflowing with injured.

Several people with life-threatening wounds were taken by helicopter to Tucson and Phoenix.

"It was a scene in there," said Gary Wendter, an emergency medical technician with the Sierra Vista Fire Department. "Blood all over. I can't begin to even describe it. I mean, it was awful. I don't know why someone would do something like this. Sick."

Sierra Vista Police Department spokesman Lt. Steve Montan said the identity of the gunman was being withheld pending notification of the next of kin. He added that an investigation into the motive was continuing.

That was it? Hell, I could have written that.

Sarah remembered the news conference. She went into Jim's office and told him she was going.

He said he would send Stan.

"I should go," Sarah said. "Stan—he's not… good."

"The presses are almost ready to roll."

"But…"

"Sarah," Smith said, rolling his eyes toward the ceiling.

"Gentleman rolled his eyes at me. Being a lady, I rolled them back," Sarah said.

Here I was looking for serious answers, and it looked like I had wandered into a road show version of *His Girl Friday*.

"You're in a good mood for someone who just came from a mass shooting," Jim said.

"Just stoked," she said.

"Stan's got the news conference."

"It's my story, Jim. If Stan goes, then it's going to get all messed up."

"Actually, Sarah, this is everyone's story. You know who's coming here today? Everyfuckingbody! The *New York Times*, NBC Nightly News, CBS, *Hard Copy*. Every idiot with a camcorder has set their sights on coming here and getting a piece of this story. Armies of reporters are, right now, descending like locusts on Egypt in the good old days. They're going to make the landing at Normandy look like a goddamn Elk's Club picnic.

"But this is our town. It's going to be our story. What I need from you is some cooperation. Is that okay with you? Do you approve?"

Sarah nodded.

"The presses roll in fifteen."

It was incredible to me the way information was shaped and communicated. They could have used a dartboard, for all the thought that went into it.

"Okay, Jim. I'm going to the news conference."

"Fine, Sarah. I have no energy. Suit yourself."

"You look like you need to be cheered up. I have a surprise. I was inside the restaurant. I got in right after the cops arrived."

"Write a sidebar," Smith said, not looking up. "Nothing fancy."

Nothing fancy, Sarah mouthed, sitting back at her computer. I hate this place. Hey, Jim, I got an interview with the captain of the *Titanic* as it slipped beneath the waves. *Oh, neat. Give me a sidebar.*

She called NBC in Phoenix again.

⌒◌◌

At Channel 8 in Phoenix, the news director, Bob Barlow, asked the engineering chief if they could get a satellite link to their truck in Sierra Vista. Barlow was the kind of boss who craved this exchange, the working-class kind that only came with engineering guys who were serious about themselves, their equipment, their time sheets.

Here I was in the big time. TV. These guys must know what they're doing. I hoped this would go better, and I might actually learn something.

"It's a million-dollar truck," the engineering chief said. "We can do it. But you got to do it soon. Something major going on?"

"Big shooting, maybe. Cell phone lines are jammed. I haven't talked to anyone there. I don't want to book time on the satellite if it's only one person dead. That's not worth it. Mike and John have to check in via pay phone."

"The gospel according to Mike and John."

"We'll have to wait, then."

Barlow looked at the engineering chief, then at the floor.

"I wonder if anyone else is there yet," Barlow said. "Maybe Channel Six. Bastards. I'd like to get this for the ten o'clock."

"It's almost nine-thirty. I don't see how. But you never know. Not in this business, you don't."

"Yes. It's that kind of business, isn't it. Keeps you hopping."

"Keeps you guessing."

"Keeps you running. I could have been a doctor, but no," Barlow said. "Lots of money in corporate PR."

"I could have worked for a major corporation," the engineering chief said. "Better benefits. Easier hours."

"Can we get the shot from Sierra Vista or not?" Barlow said.

"We have the technology," the engineering chief said. "The software. The people to man and run it."

"We have the hardware."

"Channel Six sucks. They have theme music for murders."

"We have the software," Barlow said.

"We can get a picture up in three minutes," the engineering chief said. "They aim the dish, and we'll see them. It's a matter of minutes now. A game of inches."

"We need to grab the viewers' attention."

"A whole bunch of people shot dead should take care of that."

"You would think. But we need more."

"More?"

"Let's play it like they're already there," Barlow said. "We won't wait for the home viewer. I don't want an intro. We'll break in on programming. Special report interruption."

"Those gave me chills when I was a kid. Them breaking in like the world was ending. That's some kind of action."

"We'll do a special report interruption in the middle of the news," Barlow said. "I'll call graphics."

"I like it," the engineering chief said. "It's very wake-the-neighbors. Never been done."

"We'd be breaking new ground here."

"What if it's just two or three dead?"

"Doesn't matter. We tell them early reports indicate. Sources close to the investigation say. The scene is developing. We're there. Stay tuned. You—speaking now of the home viewer—will be informed of the latest."

"I'll get you the pictures."

"I'll book time on the satellite," Barlow said. "We're going live."

"We have the technology."

"We have the software. We have the hardware. We have the...know-ware!"

"The nowhere?"

"No. the K-N-O-W-ware."

"We could use that. T-shirts. Paint it on the sides of the trucks. Baseball caps. The Know-ware. Know-ware is the news better. I like it."

"I could have gone into advertising," Barlow said.

"*Fuckwad,*" the engineering chief said.

"Fuckwad?" Barlow said.

"No, *Fuckwad.* That's the name of my kid's maga-zine. Sixteen years old, and he's a publisher. On the internet. He has a magazine. A blog, they call it."

"It's amazing what kids can do these days," Barlow said.

"He calls it *Fuckwad* because every issue he profiles a fuckwad. Like a politician."

"Isn't that something."

"I'm thinking this guy who shot those people in Sierra Vista could be the next fuckwad."

"Sure."

"Because no matter what, this guy's got to be some kind of piece of shit, some kind of real-life fuckwad. Shooting innocent people."

"Got to be."

"I'll get with you on that later. Maybe you can talk to my kid. Pass along some tips on, you know, journal-ism."

"Love to. Anytime."

"Probably make it the best *Fuckwad* ever."

⤳

Channel 8 prepared their reporter on the scene, Mike Flahgg, for the special report.

"What are we doing here?" Flahgg asked.

"We're breaking in with a special report."

Flahgg was in front of the Pizza Man. He was fussing with his earpiece and doing a mic check, to make sure he could communicate with the studio at the NewsPlex back in Phoenix.

It was all on the fly. The action from it was gurgling in everyone's bones. This, apparently, was the kind of thing news people lived for. The crew had jumped from the satellite truck at the Pizza Man thinking *move, move, move.*

It reminded me of the police and firefighters who first arrived on the scene, only not so selfless.

"A special report in the middle of the news," Flahgg said. "Who makes this stuff up?"

Flahgg's earpiece told him what to say and where to stand. It linked him to the anchor people. It was his lifeline of information.

"We have a picture up. I can see you," the studio said to Flahgg. "We're three minutes out from going live. You will be cued with 'Our Mike Flahgg has arrived on the scene at a grisly shooting in the town of Sierra Vista. He joins us now with an exclusive special report.'"

"How many dead?" Flahgg asked the studio through the microphone clipped to his tie.

"We're not sure. We're going with at least twenty, though. You're going to have to make stuff up—sources say, authorities have told me, early reports indicate. You know. But be careful."

"When in doubt, be vague," Flahgg said. "Twenty. That's a big number."

"Some kind of record."

"Then this will be picked up by the network."

"Two minutes, Mike," the studio said. "Do you have a question? What can we ask you?"

"You can ask me what the hell I'm doing here. Should I roll my sleeves up? That looks better, doesn't it? I like how that looks."

"That works. Very man-on-the-scene. What about the question?"

"He can ask me about how we're kicking Channel Six's ass on this story. Tie loose, you think? It works, right? Ask me about the people standing around here. I'll say they're in shock. Numb. Disbelieving. Tragedy in a small town, like that."

"That's good. That'll work. Thirty seconds."

"Twenty dead. Thirty seconds. What a cool fucking job this is."

⁍

"Put on Channel Eight," Sarah said to Jim. She was jumping up and down behind him in his office as he edited her story. "Channel Eight's my favorite."

"Oh, mine, too," Smith said. "They do that 'It's ten o'clock. Do you know where your children are?' Very cutting edge. Gives me goose bumps. All those child-less mothers hunkered in front of the TV awaiting word."

"*Hunkered*," Sarah said, leaning over him to switch the channel and turn the sound up, "is not a real word."

"Turn that crap down. I like what you did with the 'NO FEAR' kid. This is good. Nice detail. Turn that crap down."

"'Crap'? You *are* old. That's an old person's word. They might have something on the shooting."

"What's the kid's last name? You just have Jimmy."

"Didn't give me a last name. Refused, in fact. I asked."

"You asked."

Sarah saw Smith frown.

"Channel Eight doesn't have anything on it," Sarah said, watching the TV. "They're leading with the governor at the women's shelter."

"Next time, tip them off earlier."

"Next time," she said, "I'll call them before it happens."

"Is this a direct quote here?"

"If it's there and you see those little slashy marks around it, it's a quote."

"I should see your notes, Sarah. There isn't much here."

"We interrupt this program for an *Eyewitness News* Special Report. Live from the NewsPlex."

No one said anything. It was That Voice. That doom-sounding voice. The voice that came on maybe a few times in a lifetime. It told us the space shuttle had been reduced to bits and was raining into the ocean. It said President Reagan was shot. It told us a plane had struck the World Trade Center. And now it was talking about my shooting.

This was the early official word on my actions. In the bars and the living rooms and kitchens and basements, and in Fort Huachuca's rec room, everyone would come to a halt and be conjoined through television, conjoined by The Voice that would provide details of the terrible thing I did. Maybe *they* knew why I did it. Maybe they could tell me.

"We go now live to anchor Curt Blankenship in the NewsPlex."

"We've just learned," Curt Blankenship said soberly, "about a grisly shooting in Sierra Vista, California."

Mike Flahgg started screaming into his microphone to the studio that it was not California. Not California, *Arizona*.

"Details are sketchy at this moment, but early reports indicate as many as twenty people—quite possibly more—have been shot to death in a restaurant there. Our own Mike Flahgg is standing by live at the scene. Mike, what can you tell us?"

"Curt," he said, "police in this peaceful town in Arizona, which is home to many of our brave men and women in the armed forces, have sealed off the Pizza Man restaurant. You can see the Pizza Man behind me. It's where there has been a shooting—a mass murder, if you will. Authorities are not saying much, so I can only pass on what little information we know at this hour."

"Mike," Flahgg heard the producer say in his ear, "we have two minutes to fill. Milk it, buddy."

Then Flahgg heard Curt Blankenship say, "I really said California? It's not California? How am I supposed to know all this?"

"There are at least twenty people dead today," Flahgg said into the camera. "They were enjoying a Memorial Day holiday meal here at this popular eating spot when…as I say, details are sketchy."

"Tell us what you do know," the producer told Flahgg. "No more 'sketchy'"

"At about three this afternoon a man walked in and, for reasons still unclear, started shooting."

"Talk about the soldiers from the fort being called out," the producer said.

"Police from all over the region responded, along with soldiers from Fort Huachuca, to the scene."

"Talk about the scene, Mike."

"As you can see from where I am now standing…"

Behind Flahgg, about ten people came to life when the bright television light came on. Two kids gave the "We're #1" finger-signal, like football players on the sidelines caught in front of a camera.

"It's chaos here," Flahgg said. "People in shock. As you can plainly see. Emergency crews are here sorting out the mess, treating the wounded at local hospitals."

"Hi, Mom," a guy shouted.

"It's like a battle zone here," Flahgg said. "Total carnage. Simply awful. People standing around in obvious shock."

"Cue Curt," the producer said. "Curt, you're live."

"Mike," Curt said. "have police told you who did the shooting? Are they saying yet who did it?"

"No, Curt," Flahgg said. "They're investigating to determine the identity of the shooter. Several officers said they could not comment on that at this stage of the investigation."

"Mike, we have only a few seconds here. How are the residents reacting to this tragedy?"

"Well," Flahgg said in front of the gesturing kids in the crowd, "while it's still too early to tell, most of the people we've encountered appear, well, numb. They're stunned."

"Ten seconds," the producer said in Flahgg's ear.

"They are obviously struggling to understand why this happened in their peaceful town. This is a tragedy, one they might never get over."

"Mike, do they know why the shooting occurred?" Curt Blankenship asked.

"Why?" Flahgg said. "Why? Curt, there is no apparent motive at this time. No one knows. For *Eyewitness News*, I'm Mike Flahgg reporting live at the scene. Now, back to you in the studio."

"We're clear," the producer said. "Good job, Mike. Really nice. Kicked butt. Nina, when we come back to the regular news, I want you to start like you're in mid-sentence on the Girl Scout Cookies story."

"And there you have it from Sierra Vista," Curt said to everyone watching at home. "That's in Arizona. As many as twenty people dead. Shot while eating pizza this Memorial Day. Police have no suspects. They are, however, investigating. Tune in tomorrow when we'll bring you more on this tragic and horrible story. For *Eyewitness News*, I'm Curt Blankenship. We return you now to our regularly scheduled programming."

The face of anchorwoman Nina Sutton came on, talking as if nothing had happened.

"...selling two thousand-dollars'-worth of cookies," she said. "It just goes to show what a little hard work can do. That's one Girl Scout who's going to have one heck of a merit badge, if she keeps this up.

"When we come back, we'll turn to sports. Jimbo, who, by the way, goes ga-ga for those chocolate mint Girl Scout Cookies, will give you all your holiday scores. Stay tuned."

Sarah and Smith leaned back from the television.

"Wow," Sarah said.

"Jesus," Smith said.

Dartboard, I thought.

"They sure scooped us," Sarah said. She was giddy over how she was responsible for it. "They got it out first. I guess that kills the extra."

"No," Smith said. "A special report in the middle of the news. Big deal, doesn't change a thing. We'll do it better, that's all. Write me up that first-hand account. I need it five minutes ago. We roll presses in ten minutes."

"I don't see what good it'll do," Sarah said walking around Smith's little office. "We got scooped."

Smith leaned back and looked at her.

"Wasn't that report incredible?" she said. "The way they broke in and everything? I mean, think about it. Right here this happens. Right here, of all places, and in Phoenix, they're on it like stink on a monkey. Amazing. Power of the press."

"The power of you tipping them off," Smith said.

"I overheard someone say," Sarah said, ignoring him, "that our shooter-guy—Sam Tryor, right?—tried out for a play and didn't get the part."

"We can only hope it was *Death of a Salesman*," Smith said.

Sarah didn't laugh.

"I don't think it was," Sarah said. "Although, it could have been. I think it was *The Bird Man of Alcatraz*. Either way, it's funny, though. Death. Salesman. I get it. But this guy says Tryor was, like, majorly agitated he didn't get a part in the play. I should do more on this."

"Good. We'll need that. If he auditioned to be a road company version of Willy Loman it would explain everything."

"If it's true about him doing that, I have this great idea to call him the Bad Actor Murderer. Do you love it?"

"I love it," Smith said. He really thought Sarah was having a full-on meltdown of some sort. "That might fit with what I have in mind for you."

"No more Pizza Man shooting," Sarah said suddenly. "I'll do the news conference, and that's it."

"That's it?"

"It'll be old news by tomorrow, anyway. Bang-bang. Bang-bang-bang, and they shot two friends, and so on and so on. Besides, I have to go to Phoenix tomorrow. It's personal. I wanted to let you know."

"Here's what I want you to do," Smith said. "First, calm down. Second, listen. You're doing a story on who this guy was. I want you to talk to his family, friends, the cops, neighbors, people he worked with. Anyone. Everyone. I'm told he was a member of the Chamber of Commerce and a real pillar of the community. Find out about it. Who was Sam Tryor? That's what I want. By tomorrow night."

"But...Phoenix."

"Go. Don't go. Story. Done. Tomorrow."

"Jim."

"Sarah."

"I don't think you understand."

"I don't think you think I understand, but believe me, I understand."

"No, Jim. First off—Who gives a shit who Sam Tryor was?"

 ⚬⚬

That was when I realized— Sarah knew. She *knew* why I shot those people. She didn't know the specifics. If she had, she would have used that the same way she used her body. She knew the bigger reason, though. She knew about people the way I knew about people. She knew just how mean and stupid people could be. The difference was, I learned it late in life, and she came to it very young.

 ⚬⚬

Sarah was five when her parents dropped her off one day for a visit with her aunt Pat and uncle Sal. Her parents never came back for her. She stayed with her aunt and uncle for thirteen years.

Sarah was only marginally better off with Pat and Sal. They paid the bills and bought the booze with Sal's disability checks, and by holding a never-ending yard sale each weekend at their house in Brewster, a tough little town with tough little people about an hour outside New York. It had a train station where Sal would stand twice a week to go on "business trips" to the city. He would walk Riverside Drive or go through the streets of the Upper West side on trash days and pick through the stuff rich people threw out. Then, two times a week, except for when there was snow in the yard, they would put out the battered goods Sal had gathered.

Sal was king of a castle that had been foreclosed. He just sat on the lawn and occasionally grunted between sips from his can of Rheingold. Tourists off the train for a day in the countryside would come by the yard sale, perhaps expecting to find a Picasso behind a velvet *Dogs Playing Poker*.

Aunt Pat did her best to make up for Sal's lack of social graces with energy and enthusiasm. She chatted up each set of salt-and-pepper shakers and every waffle iron like she was working the back vault at Tiffany's.

While she was unloading Holiday Inn ashtrays into the hands of out-of-towners, Aunt Pat was also busy with her plan. Over the years, she managed to put away some coins and some cash. She would pocket a fiver if she was in a feisty mood, or if Sal had worked past his fifth Rheingold. Her plans for the cash almost came to an end over the microwave.

It was a beauty. An Amana. It was abandoned on West 68th Street. Sal spotted it a block away. He walked up close to it and scooped it into his arms before anybody could pounce on him. He shook it as he walked with it. Nothing was loose. He thought he could get it to work. He was the kind of guy who thought he could build an atom smasher out of duct tape, if he'd only gotten the breaks in life.

Sarah remembered when he brought it home. It was placed on the kitchen table. They plugged it in and turned the knob. It hummed. They turned it off. The bell rang. They nuked a potato and waited and watched. Then they ate it.

"Why'd it get thrown out? It works," Sarah said.

Sal peered in, squinting like a pro.

"Bulb's burnt! They threw it out because the bulb don't work. How do you like that?"

"Their waste is our want then," Aunt Pat said.

It went on sale two days later. This was Pat's big score, the haul that would put her plan into action. But she had to get past Sal. So, she recruited Sarah.

"Honey, you ever want something real bad?" she asked. "Something you probably can't get right off, so you take time and you plan for it, and then it comes closer and closer to being real?"

"No."

"Well, one day you will. Me, I got a thing I been planning, and I'm real close to getting it. I can get it if I sell the microwave and keep the money. So, you got to keep Uncle Sal from knowing. If he finds out I kept the money he'll want it, and I won't get my thing. And if you want something real bad you should be able to have it."

"What thing?"

"I'll tell you if I get the money. You in with me?"

They arranged a signal. When the signal was given, Sarah would fall down, skin her knee and Sal would help her clean it up.

The next day at the yard sale, Aunt Pat was talking to a man by the microwave. After a few moments, Pat gave the signal and slapped her fist into her hand. Sarah made her move. She walked around, looking at this and that, until she was out of Sal's direct sight. Then she went down. She held her left knee and said, "Ow ow ow."

"Pat. Huh. Hey, Pat," Sal said. "The kid fell. Check her out, will ya?"

"I'm busy," Pat said, making the motions of a fish on the line to Sal.

"Huh?"

She made the cast-and-reel gesture again.

"Oh, right."

Sal went over to Sarah.

"I think I hurt it real bad," she said, looking over his shoulder at Pat, who looked ready to close the deal.

"Well," he said, "what the hell did you do? Did you fall down?"

"Yeah."

"All right." Sal looked around dumbly. "Let's get you in the house, and Pat can clean that up."

"You do it! I want you to do it!" Sarah wailed. She looked over and saw that Pat was out of the yard with the customer, and the microwave was off the table.

Sal helped her into the kitchen. She scooted up to sit on the counter, and he put a wet paper towel on her knee.

"All better?" Sal asked. "No? When I was in the navy all we had was wet paper towels and we got skinned knees all the time. They always fixed me right up. Really."

"I don't believe you. I think you're lying," Sarah said, stalling.

"We also had us a bit of the hair of the dog what bit us. As a matter of fact..." Sal looked around as if he were plotting to pass state secrets. "...we could split a cold one. That would perk you up."

It tasted funny. It was either the beer, or the way Sal had his hand on her thigh very high up, and moving higher, that made her dizzy.

"Now, just don't tell your aunt about this. She'd have a flying fit," Sal said with a wink.

Sarah sat with her first beer, after having been felt up for the first time, and she wasn't sure if she wasn't supposed to tell about the beer, the grope, or what.

When they got back to the yard, Pat was packing stuff away. She looked distraught and was wringing her hands.

"Sally," she said, "now, don't get all mad or nothing like you do, but someone stole the stove. I've looked all over, and it just ain't here. And I ain't saying who done it, but there was this guy and I was talking to him and he was saying how he wanted it and I turned my back on him and now it's gone."

Sal didn't say anything. He sat back on his chair and sipped his beer and stared. You could tell, though, the world had flattened him a little bit more.

That night Sarah heard them yelling. Sal said Pat stole the money and he didn't want to hear any more about it. Pat said very little. Sarah was hoping Aunt Pat would hold firm and not tell about the plan. She put pillows over her ears.

If you want something bad enough, you should be able to have it. You should have it, Sarah remembered her aunt saying. She imagined Aunt Pat's plan was a getaway. *Aunt Pat's going to run away and she's going to take me with her because I helped. Maybe we can go to where Mom and Dad are.* That night, Sarah packed her things.

The next day Sal, went to New York to find another microwave. Sarah had her bag ready. Half an hour later, a truck arrived. Sarah figured it was a moving van. She waited inside, ready to leave.

"Oh, honey, come see!" Pat said after a while.

This is it, Sarah thought, grab a last look.

There were long green slats laid out in the yard.

"What is it?" she asked.

"Siding, honey. Ain't it wonderful? Aluminum siding!"

Sarah watched, wordlessly, as workmen put siding on the house. She knew, right then, what people are capable of, and she would carry it with her for the rest of her life. She took it as a hard lesson, but she made the best of it for herself.

Perhaps I made the worst of it.

❦

"Let me tell you about Sam Tryor," Sarah said to Jim. "Get your notepad out. Sam Tryor is another nut case who didn't get the right topping on his pizza and went ballistic. It happens every day."

"Happens every day. This happens every day? Excuse me for a second."

Smith got up and paced around outside, trying to calm down. He came back and started a speech the minute he was through the door.

"Maybe in the big, bad East, in Washington and New York and whatever other town you lived in for five months, this happens every day," he said. "Not here. This is a small town. This is a boring, nothing-happening Arizona town. People play golf. They go to church on Sunday. They don't live like perfect Christians, but they go and they put their change in those March of Dimes canisters at the store, and they buy Apple computers with their register receipts for the high school, and they tear up when they see the end of *The Sound of Music*. They do all that right here. Happens every day. But I guess you've seen eighteen bazillion murders on television already, so what's thirty or forty more in real life, right?"

I could tell Sarah did not want to have this conversation with Jim. She probably hoped that, after she got the job in Phoenix, she could come back, and they could have a drink together and hash out their philosophical differences in a philosophical way, perhaps at a piano bar in a hotel somewhere. But you can't always pick these things, and once you get going, you can't usually stop.

"Don't you start on me with that soulless younger generation shit," Sarah said. "This is a great little town. Christian, God-fearing, curing polio or scoliosis or cleft palates or whatever with their laundry money. But it's also where the big factory mixes the special color of paint for Stealth bombers and where the army trains spies. You know what I saw the other day? A personalized license plate that said X-DOUBLE-OH-SEVEN. I'm sure that guy was a real successful spy.

"Anyway. I'm making a speech. Any second I'll sound like you. God help me. Got a cigarette? Thanks. Listen, Jim. Aside from all that, I don't think this Tryor guy is going to get all that interesting. You know?"

"I don't know. Clue me."

"He's either got a bummer of a marriage..."

"Never been hitched."

"... a terminal illness..."

"I'm checking on that."

"...was the quiet type, kept to himself, didn't say much, a loner, seemed nice, always polite..."

"That's for you to find out and put in those little quote things I like so much."

"...or he was another whack-job, Jim. The point is, who gives a fuck?"

"The point is, I do."

"Why?"

"Why?"

"Yeah. Why do you care about this?"

"Because the guy killed forty people. He's one of our own, one of us. He *is* us. Slapping a tag like Bad Actor Murderer on the guy doesn't make him an alien from another planet. Also, we're a newspaper, and we find out things like 'Why did the cow jump over the moon?' 'Why did the cow start the big Chicago fire?' and 'Why did the man shoot all the nice people in the pizza place?'"

They both sat quietly, like a married couple resting up from battering each other before gearing up to do it some more.

She's a good reporter, Jim thought. Brat kid. Great legs. Great lips. I would kill potentially great men, in their cradles, to get with those lips. I admit it. I'm guilty. But Sarah's more than a great pair. Maybe her interview at Channel Eight will make her see how shallow it can be out there. She can't be stupid enough to think this Tryor guy's not important. It's obvious he's an important story. My four-year-old niece can see it. And she's autistic.

"Listen," Sarah said. "I'm going to say this once. Man goes nuts. Shoots a bunch of people. It's no big deal in the grand scheme of things. I have to go to Phoenix tomorrow. Let The Hoof do your story."

"What's in Phoenix?"

"It's personal."

"Think Channel Eight will hire you?"

"It's personal."

"Do the story, Sarah. I'm not asking."

"Got another cigarette?" Sarah asked. "Thanks. What do you think, Jim? There's going to be some movie-of-the-week trauma we can trace back to find the cause of this guy's spree with an automatic rifle? He saw his mother having sex with a Doberman when he was seven and that did it?"

"Yes. Doggie-style trauma in *The Bad Actor Murder*. Starring Lindsay Wagner. That's it."

"You're so old-school, Jim. You see everything like some drama with a hero and a cast of really deep characters who have reasons and who go around thinking about stuff all the time."

"Go on."

"You're so naïve. Christ. You think it's fascinating that this guy shot all those poor idiots. Now you want to delve into the reasons so we can all sleep better."

I would sleep better if I knew, I thought.

"That's me," Smith said. "And how do you see it?"

"How do I see it? Got another cigarette? Oh. It's still burning? How do I see it? It's amazing more people don't do what this guy did. I'm amazed every day that someone doesn't go ape-shit with a gun in a public place. I mean, think about it. So, we see it differently."

"You really believe that, don't you?"

"I really do. Maybe it's because I know better. I know people."

"Do a story on that, then."

"What? Why more people don't shoot more people more often?"

"Yes. Do that. That's interesting to me. Do that story."

"Sure, Jim," Sarah said stubbing out the cigarette. "I'll do that when I get back from Phoenix.

When Sarah left, it was merely a formality. Jim knew she was already gone.

I never saw her again.

— 9 —

*T*hree years after he killed himself, Ricardo Alfonso Cerna is still reminding deputies at the San Bernardino Sheriff's Department to check suspects for guns.

"Check your suspects. Check for guns," he whispers in deputies' ears as they prepare to interrogate suspects, or as they search suspects before putting them in a cell. Then he laughs.

On December 19, 2003, Ricardo was stopped for speeding in Muscoy, California. He took off, was chased by the police, and shot one of the officers in the stomach before he was captured. They brought him to the sheriff's office and put him in an interrogation room. It was a small room with a metal table and a chair.

Bobby Dean, the head of the department's homicide unit, came in and put his keys on the little table, handed Ricardo a bottle of water and left for a moment. For just a second, really. He left the door open, and while he was in the hall a few feet away, Ricardo took a sip of water, put the cap back on the bottle, pulled a .45 caliber automatic out of his pants and shot himself in the head.

Why did he shoot himself? The short answer was because the police were stupid and never patted Ricardo down. That was enough of an answer for Ricardo, who even as a ghost is not overly concerned with the more abstract questions of existence.

"Check your suspects," Ricardo's ghost warns deputies. "Check for guns. Make sure you check." Then he laughs and laughs and laughs…

༺✺༻

Officer Dave and Cortez took Nick to the police station to be questioned about me. I had a lot riding on this. If they could get him to talk then I might come a lot closer to finding out why.

Nick sat in the police car behind a metal mesh barrier that separated him from the front seat. He heard snippets of what Cortez and Officer Dave said up front.

"… a little tart."

"…stick this guy…"

" with my gun drawn. Yeah…"

"…so I says, 'Up against the wall, savage…'"

"…big son of a…"

Nick saw a van with a handicapped vanity plate that read "2 BAD."

What was too bad? Was it too bad because he couldn't walk or too bad because he could park close to the store in handicapped spaces and others couldn't? The ride to the station was taking a long time. Again, Nick considered the lack of handles on the inside of his door.

People say about the dead, "Doesn't make a difference to him, he's dead." As a dead person, let me just say, some things make a difference. If I knew why I'd killed forty people, it would have made all the difference to me. Don't ask me how, I just knew it would.

The need to know why came to me, settled on me and comforted me like a warm blanket on a cold, rainy day.

I didn't want to know so I could justify it, or come out of it as the good guy. I just had a need to know. With that thought, I had a breakthrough. I remembered something—finding out why was what I used to do for a living.

I worked intelligence for the School for the Americas, and my job was to figure out why. I worked the Chile desk, then the Cuba desk. I took raw data, studied it, broke it down into patterns and let those patterns tell me why Cuba and Chile were moving in one direction or another. Once we knew why something happened, we could figure out why something else was likely or unlikely to happen. That gave us a key to running other countries in the way we preferred.

My entire job was to know why something happened because knowing why gives you insight into how an entire society operates, into its strengths and weaknesses, its reasons, its soul.

If nothing else, I had to track down why I did what I did because nothing else was working for me. I had struggled and failed to remember the shooting. I also came up empty on anything about my life in any detail. Everything I remembered for sure—driving out from Detroit and the rest of it—had been filtered through Nicky. Some hazy recollections were coming through on my own, but *hazy* was the operative word.

Did I once knock on the door of our childhood home in Detroit and go in and look around? Or did I always mean to do that and just thought I had? Did I kiss Doris Eikenger in the third grade and did we promise to be boyfriend and girlfriend, or did I imagine that and made it real only in my head? Did I have a math class in high school that I never went to and showed up to only take the final, or was that a dream?

I gave up on all that and focused on finding out what put the guns in my hand at the Pizza Man. Nick and Perry were the guys who could tell me. It must have been the reason I was with them. If Perry was going to pump Nick for information about me, that was good. It gave me a chance to get to the bottom of who I was and what I did.

Something would come out of the interrogation. I just hoped they wouldn't be too rough on my brother. Because, even though I was dead, he made a big difference to me.

Before they got to the questions, though, Nick had to ID me.

◦◀▬◦

The police car pulled into the parking lot and slowed to a crawl. They were at a side entrance to the police station, away from reporters. Dave and Cortez stopped talking when the car stopped.

A man in a suit came out of the station and opened a heavy metal door halfway. He nodded at Ralph and Dave, then looked down a hall before he opened the door fully and signaled for them to bring Nick in.

The two policemen fumbled around and reattached equipment that was too clumsy to wear in the cruiser—nightsticks, mace, cuffs, stuff that clinked together. Then, at the exact same moment, they put their police hats on. Cortez smoothed the creases. Dave opened his door.

He has handles on *his* door, Nick thought.

Cortez turned and looked at Nick through the wire mesh. Nick must have looked like a dog at the pound.

"I want to say," Cortez said, "this is a big mess here. You better get yourself a good lawyer, pal. You're going to need it."

He nodded at Nick.

Is he speaking to me? Nick thought.

"And I know why. I know all about your brother and his kind. That's right. Keep looking at me like you don't hear."

Dave stuck his head back in the car, looked at Nick, then at Cortez.

"Ralph, let's get going, already. You look great."

"Yeah," Cortez said to Dave, but with his eyes still on Nick. "I was telling our friend here about how he's not going to get away with it."

"What are you talking about, Ralph?" Dave said.

"It's all this Dr. William Pierce shit. The guy who wrote the *Turner Diaries*. You've heard of him, right? Tim McVeigh's little training manual on how to bomb the Federal Building? He read it back when he was living in Kingman. That's right. The Viper Militia? All these types coming to Arizona. Arab flight students. You picked the wrong town in Arizona today, buddy. No flight schools here."

This cop's nuts, Nick thought.

"Ralph! Don't be a fucking idiot," Dave said. "Get the guy. Let's go."

I'm not cuffed, Nick thought. I could run when they open the door. Kick it and take off. Head to the hills. They got caves up there. Drink from the puddles, eat leaves.

"Watch your head, Mr. Tryor."

Cortez gripped his hand around Nick's arm tightly. He led him through the doorway then down a hall. The air conditioning inside made Nick realize it had been boiling hot outside. Cortez's grip hurt. His fingers went numb from Cortez's fingertips digging into his brachial artery. He didn't say anything.

"You taking Debbie to the party tonight?" Dave asked Cortez as they led my brother along.

"She's got to work."

"It's Memorial Day. Well, they'll probably cancel the party. What with all."

"Mr. Tryor, we're going to ask you to remain here for a moment," Cortez said.

Dave and Cortez nodded to one another, and Dave went into a room and closed the door behind him.

Nick stood in the hallway and made sure not to look at Cortez

"It'll be a moment," Cortez said. He shot Nick a look and put his hand on his service revolver.

A woman came down the hallway.

"Lil, I got Mr. Tryor here."

Cortez and Lil moved a few steps away to speak.

Cops and doctors, Nick thought. They always talk about you, and they don't let you hear.

"What am I supposed to do with the guy?" Cortez said to Lil. "Where do we put him?"

"Keep your voice down, Ralph."

Nick stared at the linoleum. He felt embarrassed to be a bother.

"Where's he *supposed* to go?" Cortez said. "You tell me, because I'm not babysitting this guy."

"Put him in the chief's office. Perry can talk to him there."

"Mr. Tryor, we're going to have you wait in Chief Samson's office for the time being," Cortez said. "We don't have any interview rooms free, and that's what we're going to do."

The hand clamped back down on the arm and the artery, and Nick was led to an office.

⌒≈◌

I thought about the accused, about how the accused always look. They are led and held, and no one speaks near them, yet everyone stands close to them. The men in suits and uniforms grip the accused. They always clench something attached to the accused, or to his leg or arm.

And as they are led, probably *because* they are being led, the accused look mean. Led in or out, photographers at bay, they shuffle along. They wear shackles. They hear the accusations. They radiate a caged power as they shuffle along in their baby steps. They don't have expressions. They rarely smile. If they do smile, they only look meaner. There's no way for them to communicate their humanity. They fulfill all expectations of what a criminal should look like, and they are only accused. Take one look and you know it—the worst must be true.

That was how they were treating my brother, and that was what he looked like, and he didn't do a goddamned thing.

☙❧

The chief's office had a big chair behind a big polished desk. Citations, certificates and plaques—DARE To Keep Kids Off Drugs, DUI Task Force of Southern Arizona, Citizen's Patrol, City Council Man of the Month—covered every inch of every wall.

"Lieutenant Perry will be in to speak with you shortly," Cortez said. "There are things I have to do, but I'll keep this door open and I'll be in to check on you."

"Thank you, Officer," Nick said before he sat down slowly onto the chair in front of the big desk. "Can I ask you a question, though?"

"Yes, you can."

"My brother," he said in a squeaky voice before clearing his throat. "Where's my brother?"

"Wait here for Lieutenant Perry. He'll be along shortly."

"Thank you."

Left alone, Nick exhaled for what seemed like ten minutes. Everything started to catch up to him. Possibilities crashed around in his brain. He couldn't have that. He was nuts. He was bolts. He pulled it together as best he could.

I'm in a police station waiting to talk to a lieutenant, he thought. I'm in the chief of police's office here in Sierra Vista. It's a Monday. The door is open. Did I lock the door at home? I have my keys. It's strange to touch them. Breathe.

Sam. We would sit in a bar and talk about how if the other died then we would be alone. Did I leave the coffee machine on at home? Where is Sam? I hope the front porch light is on. It's ten minutes past five o'clock. We were so dramatic when we talked about one of us dying. Sometimes we would call each other to say "I had this thought." And sometimes I thought, *Sam's dead.*

Nick knew the day Mom died that someone close to him was dead. He was riding in a car with a friend, and he turned to him and said, "Someone's dead. I know it." Then, an hour later, I called him and told him about Mom.

At the chief's desk, Nick gave in and bent over. He covered his face with his hands then put his hands on his knees, and he thought, with complete and accurate certainty, Sam's dead. Sam's dead. Sam's dead. Sam's dead.

☙

Perry reminded himself he'd gotten a memo, and that now they called it an interview. They don't call it an interrogation anymore. A suspect interview. *Interrogation* sounded too much like the single bulb hanging, the whack of the hose or rolled quarters in a sock wrapped around the hand. *Questioning* was still used, but it was on its way out. Perry reminded himself he was going to conduct an "informational interview" with my brother.

"Bev, what have we got?" he asked the dispatcher, who also worked the phones.

"We've got a mess," Bev said, pressing a button and connecting a caller with a cop. "We have a big, fat mess. Reporters everywhere. People calling like crazy. I had to call two more dispatchers in. Holiday pay, too. We're swamped. Everyone wants to know everything. I'm having trouble staying polite on the phone. You seen the chief?"

"Nope. Where's our guy?"

"Our guy," Bev said, "Which one's our guy again?"

"Okay."

∽◉∾

The lobby of the police station was noisy and tense and packed with people. Some were family members of those who had been killed or people whose loved ones were missing. They looked like they were set for a siege, like they were there for the long haul. They had water bottles and pillows. They wanted information, and they were not leaving until they got some.

Inside the chief's office, where Nick waited, was like any other day—quiet, serene and administrative.

Perry looked down the hallway and saw Cortez standing sentry. He stood stiff-backed and serious in front of the chief's office.

"What have we got, Ralph?"

Ralph filled him in. He never looked Perry in his eyes. Instead, he stared straight at the wall, like an imitation of every marine guard in every movie he'd ever seen.

"Has this guy been told?"

"Told?" Cortez said, with no clue what Perry was asking him. "Told what?"

"Go away, Ralph. Go clean your gun or something. Have we started any paper on this guy?"

"I didn't," Cortez said, confused. "No. Do you want me to?"

"Go away."

Perry looked at the chief's door with Nick behind it. The truth was, Perry was good at telling people the worst news. He could make the phone call, or stand face-to-face, deliver the hard news and not flinch. *There's been an accident*, he would say. Or *Your son was in the wrong place at the wrong time*. He also used *She died instantly*, and *I don't think he was in any pain*. It was a skill, but still, he hated it.

He slid a blank report sheet onto a clipboard. He wrote the name "Nick Tryor" in the spot for *name*. He left the other spaces—age, Social Security number, address, time of incident, charges, narrative of incident—blank.

For a second, he thought, I could just fill out this form and never talk to him. That's what we'll do. Just fill out the paperwork, make new files, leave the guy there and go home.

He pictured Nick sitting in the chief's office for years waiting to be interviewed. Cops would slip minute steaks, saltines and the occasional newspaper under the door to him. His beard would grow, his clothes would get ragged, his teeth would end up piled in a corner of the room, and he would mutter to himself like an old gold miner in a ghost town looking for his mule.

Perry put his hand on the doorknob then stopped. Before he went in, he decided, he should call the morgue. It was best to make sure.

"Sam Tryor? Tryor? Tryor? He's here," the morgue attendant said. "Yes, we have him in a drawer. We don't put them on hooks anymore, officer. But I have to tell you, it's been a hell of a day."

In the background, over the phone, Perry heard a song. It was Sinatra. That's Sinatra, he thought. I like Frank. What's the song? It's a younger Frank. What the hell is it?

"There are bodies stacked up," the attendant said. "I mean that literally. We are stacking them."

The music, Perry thought, I know this song.

"Is there anything else, officer? Hello?"

"Thanks," Perry said. "Hey, what's that song playing?"

"Song? Hell if I know," he said. "I can't hear it too well. The corpses really muffle the sound."

◦◦◦

Nick heard the knock and the doorknob turn. This is it, he thought. The news. Some answers. He wondered how to act.

"Mr. Tryor. I'm Lieutenant Walter Perry with the Sierra Vista Police Department."

Perry sat down and looked at the clipboard with the name and nothing else on it. He looked at the blank spaces and thought about the song in the morgue. He knew Nick was scared, but he acted official instead of comforting.

"Are you Sam Tryor?" Perry asked.

"I'm *Nick* Tryor," Nick said, getting to his feet, confused. "Sam's my brother. Is he all right?"

"Nick!" Perry yelled, correcting himself. "Nick Tryor. That's what I meant to say. Please, sit down, Mr. Tryor."

Nick sat back down and watched Perry stare at the blank report. If he was a doctor, and I was in a maternity waiting room, this would be bad, Nick thought. When it's good news they come out of swinging doors

117

and they say *Congratulations! It's a bouncing baby boy*—or girl. They bounce, those babies. When it's bad news, when the kid has a defect, is missing fingers or toes, has a disease, has no discernible sex, they say *Please, sit down.*

Perry put the clipboard on the desk and folded his hands together over it. He wondered, What the hell is that song?

"Mr. Tryor, I have some bad news," he said.

"Bad news."

"Your brother Sam died earlier today. There was a shooting at a restaurant, and he was there. I'm sorry to have to tell you."

Nick took it well. He swallowed hard and said, for God knows what reason, "Thank you."

On the other hand, I felt like I would throw up. I kept hearing I was dead. I pictured a chunk of my head gone. I was dead. I wanted to understand why. I wanted to hug my brother. I was dead. There was a shooting at a restaurant, and I was there. What the hell? What the hell? I was dead.

Perry felt both better and sick after he got the words out. He pushed on.

"I know this is difficult," he said, "but I need you to come with me. To identify the body. It's important, or I wouldn't ask."

"Of course," Nick said.

"If there's anyone you need to call, or anyone I can call for you…"

"Thank you," Nick said again, politely and inappropriately.

They didn't say anything on the way to the morgue, four blocks away. A few times, Nick looked like he was about to talk, but he didn't. He thought there was more bad news coming from this guy, and he braced for it.

Perry drove and thought about the song in the morgue. He seemed grateful to be on the move, doing something.

The evening was cool and mellow. A wind started to whip up, the sweet smell of rain was on the breeze. They got to the two-story building and took an elevator down to the basement.

Why aren't I crying? Nick thought in the elevator. This is life and death and the eternal questions and tragedy. Right here and right now. Me, a cop, the morgue, Sam dead. I'm so calm. Maybe I'm in shock. I've read about this. It's one of those things everyone's read about.

"Ramon," Perry said to a young, handsome, tattooed Hispanic man in a lab coat with the sleeves rolled up. "We need to get a look at Tryor."

"Tryor, right," Ramon said in a normal voice volume that, in comparison to Perry's funereal tone, made it sound like he was yelling his head off. "It's going to take a minute. We been real busy today."

"I understand," Perry said.

"Normally, it's not like this," Ramon said. "Usually, it's no waiting. You ask, we deliver, you know? But, man, I don't know. Lots of people up and died today. We got them in the hospital like you wouldn't believe. I know the holidays are usually busy, but, Lieutenant, I'm telling you, it's crazy."

"Ramon?" Perry said, leaning in close so Nick couldn't hear. "We had a shooting today."

"No shit? I had no idea," Ramon said. "These dead people are all from the same place? Same thing?"

"Yes."

"This is some kind of record, isn't it?"

"Yes." Perry looked around for the guy's boss. He didn't see anyone.

"What was it? Like, a mob hit? Man, mob hits. Arizona mob hits. Unreal."

"Could we please do this without speaking," Perry said.

"Who done it? Some whack-job? Some nut case, eh? Some guy from out of town? Who else would? Jesus, I mean…the people here. They leave the city to get away from this, right? Did you get the guy? Is this the guy?" He looked at Nick like he was a piece of furniture. "Or is this your partner? Was that my bad?"

"Tryor. I need to see him. Now."

The area where Perry listened to Ramon's theories of mass assassination was at the hub of a wheel. There were four white-tiled hallways that led off it, like spokes. Nick wandered away from Ramon and Perry and went down one of the halls.

There were dead bodies covered in sheets along the walls. They were mute, still and real. They lay there matter-of-factly. They didn't look like they were sleeping or napping or about to get up and do anything. They didn't look anything but dead. Dead under that pale white civil-service light looked like nothing but dead.

The only way you could tell the bodies apart was by the numbers they'd put on them. I tried to count them, but I lost my place twice and had to start over. I counted twenty-seven, and then the numbers in that particular hallway stopped.

Perry came down the hall, got Nick and gently brought him back to the hub. Ramon showed them through a door. Beyond the door was a room so small it looked stunted, like it was stuffed into the building. There were floor-to-ceiling steel doors on one wall of the cold, tight room. They were morgue drawers. There was a dead person behind each door.

The doors looked like the compartments in an ice cream truck. They had the same handles and catches on the handles. Perry looked away from the stack of drawers. He looked out-of-place, about to show a man his dead brother who was a murderer, and who wore a funny tie.

What is that song? he wondered.

"We're waiting. Someone will be here in a moment," Perry said to Nick, who tapped his finger manically against his hand, the same as when he was a kid and we were in church.

So thorough, Nick thought. This is nice. It's calm. It's efficient. The lab guy is doing his best, really. I thought he was going to say to me, We're not number one, but we do try harder!

I'm going to think about that dumb joke years from now. This policeman, he's nice, too. He's got questions, though. The questions are coming off him like heat. He's probably the one who has to question all the victims' families. That must be difficult. He tells them the news, asks them if he can get anything for them, then he asks them for bits of personal information. *Even the most obscure detail might help us solve this baffling case*, he might say. *Feel free to share, to grieve. Can I get you a refill?* That's a hard job on a day like today. It's a hard job any day, but they're busy today.

"Hello," Ramon said. He sounded like someone had spoken to him about his previous attitude. But his attempt to act more professional and friendly made him seem like a game show host basking in the tension of the bonus round. He walked over to the wall of drawers.

"We're all set," he said. "He's in drawer twenty-three. Right here. Now, wait," he said with a check of the clipboard, "I'm told there was trauma. To the head region."

"The head region," Nick said. "What kind of trauma?"

"It doesn't contain that information here. It says only 'trauma.' I wanted to tell you, though."

121

"Trauma," Nick said. "The region of the head."

"It's a gunshot wound, Mr. Tryor," Perry said. "Your brother was shot in the head."

"Shot in the head," Nick said, looking a little wobbly. "All right. Okay. You can open it."

Ramon paused. He showed Nick and Perry an emotionally complex look like, *This is going to be grim, it's not my fault, we did all we could do.*

There was a swoosh of unseen wheels along smooth runners and a figure covered with a sheet slid out.

They have that look, thought Perry, who glanced at Nick then elsewhere to avert his entire self away from that painful, private moment. Their eyes. They twitch. The actual eyeballs twitch. Oh, shit, I know the song. I had it! Okay. Don't rush it. Work it through. You're close on this. It's Frank.

"Mr. Tryor, are you ready?" Perry said.

Nick nodded.

It wasn't like in the movies when they show bodies in the morgue. The lighting was bright, harsh, fluorescent. Nothing was like it was in the movies. The cops weren't gruff, and Nick was not about to swear revenge, and no one had their own soundtrack. It was just me with a part of my head missing, and Nick was going to look at me and say something like, "Yes, that's my dead brother. That's the place a part of head used to be."

The sheet was folded down to my waist. I was getting tired of the sight of my dead self. I wanted to see myself right before I died, when I was thinking about being dead. I had little use left for the dead me.

"Yes," Nick said.

"Mr. Tryor, is this man your brother?" Perry asked.

"Yes."

"And is his name Sam Tryor?"

"Yes, that's my brother. His name is Sam."

Nick thanked Ramon when he pulled the sheet up to my neck. After a moment, Ramon and Parry stepped across the room to let Nick alone.

Nick thought my arms were thin and knotty, like a miler's. He thought my tie was cruddy. He tried to not look at the blood in my hair from the hole in the back of my head. He noticed I had shaved today. He thought about how I hated to shave because I have sensitive skin. He thought about how I was not just sleeping, about how I was actually dead. Cold, stiff, dead, sad, Sam is how he thought of me. Nuts and bolts.

"It's a bad hand," Ramon whispered to Perry. "The guy got dealt a bad hand."

"Excuse me?" Perry said.

"That's why," Ramon said. "That's why he killed those people. See, we're all like photo negatives. We get born with this picture waiting to develop. It wasn't this guy's fault. It's chromosomes, faulty neurons."

"Really."

"Absolutely. I study this stuff in my spare time. Genetics and whatnot. It's depressing, in a way, but re-assuring, too."

"So, it's a done deal? This guy got a bad hand, and that's that?"

"Yeah," Ramon said, looking across the room at Nick. "There's no blame. It's science. Like a photo negative. You can be under- or over-exposed, but you're still the same. We should do an autopsy on this guy. Cut his brain and find out."

"Okay," Nick said loudly from across the room before he put the sheet back over my face.

For a second, with the sheet pulled over my face, Nick thought about how I wouldn't be able to see. He thought about when we were kids and we pulled the sheets up and turned a flashlight on and talked in low whispers about all the things we'd like to do that were bad.

❦

"All right," Perry said. "Thank you. Mr. Tryor. I will need to speak with you. The sooner the better. If you feel you need a lawyer, that's fine, you can call one. I'm not saying you need a lawyer. You're not in any trouble, but we need to speak. It would be best if we talked back at the station. It would be best if we did so immediately."

They were in the lobby of the building, one floor up from the morgue.

"I won't need a lawyer," Nick said as they walked to Perry's car. "I'm not in trouble. This is turning into a long day. I could use a cup of coffee. Is this about Sam?"

"Yes," Perry said as he opened the car door for Nick. He closed it. By the time he reached the fender to make the turn and go to his side of the car, he thought he had the song figured out. That itch in his brain was about to get scratched. Come on, Frank. Frank Fucking Sinatra.

But he didn't get it. A snippet of the melody lingered like a ghostly soundtrack and drove him a little more crazy.

❦

It wasn't just me and Perry who wanted to know why. The question was spreading. It was on its way to blotting out all other considerations about the shooting. Just like Perry and the chief said back in the Pizza Man, the police had to answer the question. If they didn't, then a kind of dread panic would take hold. If there was no discernible, definite, ah-ha! reason for the shooting, then the center, such as it was, might not hold.

I understood this. It was why it was important to a lot of people to make me into an "other," a nut job, a freak, an aberration with a tumor who went crazy one day and could be dismissed.

Just how important it was became obvious when Lieutenant Steve Montan had the first news conference about the shooting.

While Perry and Nick drove back to the station, Montan stood in front of the Pizza Man. His face was red and hot from the television lights. He spoke in a clipped cadence at the top of his marine-trained voice.

"This is going to be orderly, and we'll take a few questions afterward," he said. "Is that understood?"

The reporters yelled,

"What about the shooter?"

"Did you make an arrest?"

"Is there a count on the dead?"

"What about the motive?"

"What's the deal with the guy who did it?"

"Why did he do it?"

The mass of reporters was huge. There was some pushing and gouging for space near the front. People were hit upside their heads with microphones and cameras. Toes got stepped on, hair got mussed, feelings got hurt.

There were eight news stations from Phoenix and Tucson and all four TV networks plus CNN and MSNBC and whoever else. Miles of cable had been spooled out onto Fry Boulevard, which was closed in front of the restaurant. The *New York Times* and *LA Times, Arizona Republic* and a slew of other newspapers sent reporters. They all dressed like Rodney Dangerfield in red ties, white shirts and black suits. Some screwball public relations types and tabloid TV guys walked around on the periphery of the group.

"I'm going to start this news conference by reading a statement," Montan said. "I'll ask that you hold your questions until afterward."

"Does this guy have a military background?"

"Is there a terrorist connection?"

"We were told it's a hate crime."

"Was he insane?"

"Did he have a medical condition?"

"Should people avoid pizza places until you determine a motive?"

"Why did he do it?"

"Why?"

Montan ignored the questions and started to read.

"The Sierra Vista Police Department earlier today responded to a report of a shooting at the Pizza Man restaurant on Fry Boulevard, in Sierra Vista, Arizona," he said in his official voice.

The reporters wrote what he said and thought about what he didn't say, such as *Why? What the hell happened,* and *who is this guy? Why? Can we get an interview with the guy? Are there any relatives? Why? A name. We need a person attached to the hand attached to the finger on the trigger that pulled it and pulled it and pulled it.* Maybe he was ex-GI. Maybe a gangbanger proving his manhood. Maybe it was a woman. There's a twist. Most likely he's some poor schlub whose wife left him or some paramilitary, *Soldier of Fortune* magazine-reading, Arizona-grown nut job, mad because the government gives out money so welfare mothers can keep squeezing out puppies for the bucks. Whatever.

Montan spoke, and the reporters wrote down and recorded what he said. While they wrote, they also figured out the angles for their stories. Violence in small-town America was a common theme. Murder hits home. Holiday horror. Murder near a secret Fort Huachuca installation. Man goes crazy with gun at small town restaurant. Those were their emerging themes.

Why was the question, though.

"We anticipate a speedy conclusion to this investigation. In fact," Montan said, "this is open-and-shut. It should only be a matter of time before we wrap it up. In conclusion, we would like to praise the efforts of local citizens in assisting the officers at the scene. Any other information we have, we will share with you. I am now prepared to take a few questions.

"Why'd he do it?"

"What's the motive?"

"Is it terrorist-related?"

"Was the shooter in a cult?"

"What's the number on the dead?"

"One at a time," Montan said. "One at a time. A number I have been given—and this is ballpark—is forty dead. Yes, that's right—four-oh. And, yes, we have identified the shooter, who killed himself after the rampage. The shooter is a man named Sam F. Tryor. T-R-Y-O-R."

The name was flung out like a piece of meat to a pride of lions. It set off a crazed reaction. The reporters grunted, pointed, gestured and yelled.

"One at a time," Montan said, annoyed. "We have no motive at this time. We have our best people on that."

"How can you not know?" reporters asked.

"Are people safe?"

"How the hell can you not know why this man shot all these people? This is not something that happens every day."

"Did he leave a note?"

"We are working on the motive and expect to have information on that shortly," Montan lied. "Indications are that he acted alone and that he, obviously, was not in his right mind. Obviously. That's all for now. Thank you."

Voices started talking into cell phones. They told people in New York and Los Angeles that I was crazy, that I was not in my right mind, that I was a nut case. They said they would have details on my insanity and craziness and not-right-mindedness soon.

The news conference, such as it was, ended.

꩜

It was quiet in Perry's car when he and Nick drove from the morgue. The easy part was having Nick ID me. Now, it would get really tough. Perry would have to tell Nick that I shot forty people earlier that afternoon, and he would have to find out why I did it.

How do you tell someone their brother is a mass murderer? Perry thought. Why aren't I outraged? I'm sitting here with a man whose last name is like Hitler, Booth, Mengele, bin Laden. Sam Tryor's life is over, and his brother Nick's might as well be. They are going to burn him down. People are going to make life a living hell for him in Sierra Vista. I live here, too. I'm alone with the guy. I could take a clean shot.

"You piece of shit," Perry muttered about a guy in an Oldsmobile in front of him. "Where'd you get your license, box of fucking Cracker Jacks? I ought to run your license. Punk mother. Run, you…you little piece of shit. Yeah, you."

"What's that?" Nick said.

"Huh?"

"You were saying something."

"Oh, nothing. I got a song stuck in my head, and I can't remember the name."

"I hate that," Nick said.

Nick was lucky he didn't get stuck with some gung-ho, yahoo idiot whose first reaction was to hate. Lots of cops, lots of *people*, hate on reflex. They get hard and mean and justify it because life is hard. Perry was one of those guys once. Then a man he called a "sick little fucker," a man he hated right off with all his heart before he even met him, turned out to be just a sad little man with the worst luck and just the nicest guy in the world.

It happened back in Baltimore. Perry answered a call about someone dead. Neighbors had been alerted by the smell, so he'd been dead a long time. The house, when Perry arrived, was disgusting. There were two dog carcasses in one corner, decomposed. The place was littered with yellowed newspapers, old food, beer cans and bits of rusted barbed wire. There was a thick, musty odor throughout the place. A man's partly decomposed headless body lay perpendicular to, and half in, an open refrigerator. His skull was on top of the fridge.

Police were baffled. Perry and the other cops stood in the muck and tried to breathe the sludgy air through surgical masks while they swapped theories and waited for the medical examiner. They talked about it being a religious cult, cannibals, a creative mob hit. Whatever it was, it made them sick.

Then, at five-fifteen, the dead man's brother came home, lugging a six-pack of Falstaff beer. Perry put the guy in a room at the police station and got set to put it to him. But before he interrogated him, he had a question.

"How could you sleep each night in that place, that tomb?"

"My brother," the man said slowly, in an accent Perry couldn't place beyond "the Old Country," wherever the hell that was, "he die. He open the refrigerator to get beer, and he die. I leave him to work. And one day I come home. Dogs playing with him. His head. So

I put up they can't get. I don't know what to do. They want money to bury and I work driving at night to get. Not enough money. I was trying to get. Driving at night."

Perry never forgot how sad. He called someone he knew at social services to help the man, and he let the guy go after he promised to get his house cleaned. Then he went home and showered for an hour.

He also felt bad for Nick, but there was no way out—he had to tell him what I did.

"Mr. Tryor," Perry said as he drove, "I have to tell you, your brother is suspected of killing forty people in that restaurant today. We believe he then turned the gun on himself. He shot himself after killing those people."

"I see."

"I have to interview you, so we can get some answers. We need to know why he did this. We need to get to the bottom of this. I know this is difficult. It has to be done. If you want a lawyer, you can have one. It's something we have to do. If there's anything you need, please ask."

"Moreover," Nick said.

"Pardon? Moreover what?"

"Moreover the dog."

"I'm sorry, Mr. Tryor," Perry said, pulling the car into an empty space behind the police station so they could go in undetected. "I don't understand. What's 'Moveover the dog?'"

"He's Sam's dog. He's a great dog. Can we get him? He's got to be hungry. He's always hungry, and he'll have to go out. I'm thinking Sam hasn't seen to him all day. It's important. He loves that dog."

"Moreover."

"From the Bible," Sam said. "There's a sentence in the Bible that goes, 'Moreover, the dog.' It's a joke."

"Of course. I'll get Moreover myself when we're done here," Perry said, grateful for the chance to search my house. "We shouldn't be too long."

"Thank you," Nick said. "That's very kind of you."

I had a dog. Of course. Moreover was a coffee table dog—short and squat and old. He was wide enough to be a coffee table. He was a good dog, if I remember. The things that get lost and forgotten at a time like this. I hoped he was all right.

◦≈◦

They went into a standard interview room. It was a big, brightly lit room. It had a stainless steel table and four chairs. There was a large mirror on one wall. They sat down and got right to it.

"What sort of a man was your brother?" Perry asked.

"He was a nice guy," Nick said. "I'm not saying that in that cocktail party way. He was a good man. Except for today, of course."

Perry didn't say anything. He sensed Nick wanted to say more and waited for him to continue

"He was suspicious, though," Nick said. "He was guarded. In a way, that made him nicer. I'm talking a lot, huh? Sam would apologize before anyone could say the thing that would make him apologize. It made me nuts. I'd tell him, 'Don't apologize. You didn't do anything wrong.'"

"Was he a calm man?" Perry asked. "Was he nervous? Did he smoke?"

"He had a lot going on, I'd say. I'm thinking of this all right now. This is like a kind of therapy. Shock therapy, I'd say, though. Sorry. What was I saying?

"I didn't know what was going on in his head half the time. He had a warped sense of humor. I admit, I'd laugh at things he said without knowing what he was talking about. I'm not sure I got it all the time. He smoked in high school but gave it up because Doris Eikenger thought it was icky, and he liked her. A lot. He never did go out with her, though."

"Was he like you? Are you like him?"

"We're brothers. We moved out here together. We lived together. We have the same parents, the same habits. We never forgot where we were from. He, more than me. Much more. We never went back. Not even for a visit."

"Back where?" Perry asked, taking notes.

"Detroit. We're from Detroit. I'd say we're like each other, but we're not. We're each other but, like, poured through a solution first, and changed."

"Is he the kind of guy would shoot a lot of people?"

"Am I?"

Perry looked at the clock on the wall and excused himself. He said he was going to get some coffee.

He walked out of the room and paced in the hall. He put his game face on and tried to focus on the interrogation—the interview—because he knew how important it was. Nothing is trivial, he said to himself. The Son of Sam was caught because of a parking ticket. There is so much information already, and more developing every moment. Interviews, recalled facts, descriptions, timelines, relatives of friends who knew old enemies who remembered. All of it was getting collated and collected and filed. Any of it could be the most important piece of information we will get.

Perry scrambled around the station and begged, demanded, scraped and collected chips, scraps and files of information that might be useful in the interview with Nick. He knew he should have done it earlier, but he was tired and he forgot. He left Nick cooling his heels.

He spoke to a patrolwoman named Constance DeNardo. She ran down witness statements for him.

"What does 'bad day for the home team' mean?" Perry asked.

"Maybe he was some psycho baseball fan pissed about free agency and the designated hitter rule," De-Nardo said with a shrug.

"Who told you he said that?" Perry asked. "Did he yell it, mutter it, swear it, whisper it? We are trying to develop a picture of the shooter. Who is this guy? What's behind this? What was he thinking when the gun came out? What is the significance of pouring a Coke on his gun?"

"It was a Pepsi," she said.

"The final count on the dead and wounded. Is that a significant number to our man? Did he have a history with this restaurant? Did he work for them? Did he apply to work for them? Did he ever make a complaint because the cheese was burnt on the edges of a pizza?"

"I like that," DeNardo said, trying to calm Perry down.

"I like that, too," Perry said. "No one calls them pizza pies any more. Have you noticed that? Why not? Is there a history with this man and the chain of restaurants? Is there a history with the parent company of the chain of restaurants? Is there a history with the independent owner-operator of this particular restaurant? Find out and let me know.

"A man goes outside society—he kills, rapes, robs, and does other bad things. Then you have to follow his trail and assign motive. You have to. Actually, as a detective, *I* have to. You must isolate the bad guy and try to understand what lies behind the unfathomable act. If not, all is chaos and darkness. Tomorrow everyone will wonder, 'What happened?' We have to know so we can tell them so then they can say, 'Oh. Okay. Thanks. I have to get to work now and not worry.'"

Perry went to another room. As he walked, he said to himself, You must do more than merely ask questions. You must ask the correct ones in the correct order, switch between specifics and generalities. That's how you trap, trick and get them.

He found a sergeant named Jimenez and got more information about what happened during the shooting.

"So, a woman—you said a black woman?—gets up, offers to blow this guy's head off after he lays the place to waste, and he lets her walk out saying, 'Nah, I'll get it. Thanks anyway?'"

"That's what the witness said."

"Find that woman. Find her. And while you're at it, there was a kid who also left. Find him."

Perry knew the proverbial window of opportunity could slam shut at any moment. He was afraid Nick would clam up. That would be a mess. They would be left stumbling around, inventing scenarios.

Christ, I can see us, Perry thought. Making shit up. The state guys, Homeland Security—they love hypotheticals. Jesus. This case already has too many moving parts. Can't let the state guys descend hard on this town. Or Feds. They come down locust-like, they do. We have no answers yet, and this gets messy, those tall guys stalking around like Lurch. All kinds of bad.

"Whose guns are they?" Perry asked Jimenez. "You said they don't belong to the shooter. Then who? Find out who. Find that guy. I want him here five minutes ago."

☜☞

Back in the interview room, Nick was more relaxed than he had been in the chief's office. That was because it was an official room. No plaques, no insincere awards. Perfect for the task. The table, four chairs, gray carpeting, tiny skylight in the ceiling, big mirror. Perfect for Nick. The lighting was unremarkable. No shadows were cast on the white walls. There was no gum under the table—when Perry was out of the room, Nick felt around, one of many vestigial habits from grade school.

In a room such as this, Nick would answer whatever was asked.

For Nick, that's what you did. The police asked questions, and he answered. It didn't matter to him if the questions were right, wrong or mistaken. He would answer and clear everything up. He was like me, apparently, and believed in the system. He told himself to hold nothing back. He told himself to forget nothing, to be completely forthcoming. He reminded himself this was the police, and this was serious business.

᠅

"Was your brother political?" Perry said to Nick when he came back and slid a cup of coffee over to him.

"Do you mean Republicans and Democrats?"

"No, I mean, was he a gun-toting right-wing extremist abortion protester? Was he a president-hater like those radio talk show guys? Was he mad about the lack of bipartisan cooperation in Washington? Did he march for equal rights for gays or against gun control or for Black rights? Like that."

"No, nothing like that," Nick said.

"Was Sam married?"

"Divorced. She was a diphthong. That's what he called her. They were together maybe five years. He got her pregnant when he was in the army."

"Army. Here at Fort Huachuca?"

"Yes."

"Doing what?"

"Listening and figuring," Nick said. "He was a listener. He didn't talk much about it. He said he listened to the Russians telling the Cubans we were all idiots, and wrote it down. They do all that spy stuff out here. School of the Americas. Sam called it 'cloak-and-dagger.' He loved to say that—cloak-and-dagger. He'd joke about being a spy. Hiding behind cactus in the desert, spying on javalinas and sending in agents to dispatch them. That was one of those things, like a joke I didn't get. Like that."

"Was it a son or a daughter? His child with his now-divorced wife?"

"Miscarriage. He stayed with her, though. Five, six years? To apologize, I always thought."

"Mr. Tryor. I appreciate you answering these questions. It helps us. Helps us get to the bottom of this."

"The bottom. That's important, of course."

"I'm going to take you closer to today, all right? When was the last time you spoke to your brother?"

"Thursday...what's today, Monday?"

"Memorial Day. Yes."

"Then it was Thursday. For a minute. About what was going on and like that."

"And what was?"

"Going on?"

"Yes."

"Nothing."

"You spoke about nothing?"

"For a few minutes. The way you do."

"What was the nature of the nothing? Did you guys talk about sports, about baseball, what?"

"Sports. No, we're not sports guys."

"No baseball?"

"Baseball? Sam hates baseball. He says it's as exciting as watching cars rust. Hates baseball guys. The whole precise thing, you know? Stats and mitts and bats and those stupid shirts with the sleeves too short to be long and chewing tobacco and falling asleep in the stands and pine tar. The attitude repulses him. You know the one I'm talking about? Baseball is a team sport, and Sam's not a team-sports guy. Home or away, doesn't like them. He runs. He's a runner. And he swims a bit."

"And how was Sam? Was he okay? Was he depressed or angry? That you could tell. This is important."

"I understand. Depressed? Angry? Nope."

"You say Sam didn't like baseball."

"Right."

"What does it mean, 'bad day for the home team?'"

"Bad day for the home team? That's, like, 'No shit, baseball fans.' Or it's, like 'Yeah, and I want to pitch in the next World Series.'"

"I'm not following you."

"It's an expression. My mother—our mom—she was always saying stuff like that. She was a big Tigers fan back in Detroit. She saw all the games, from the bleachers. Sat there with a dog and a beer and was in heaven. And if she was, you know, having a bad day she'd say that—'Bad day for the home team.' Or if I said, 'Mom, I want a toy,' and she didn't have the money, she'd say 'Yeah, well, I want to pitch in the next World Series.' Like that."

"No shit."

"No shit, baseball fans."

"You guys grew up poor."

"Very. Not a pot, as they say. The old man drank. We had us those Salvation Army Christmases. You know?"

"I've heard."

"They'd take us to this big auditorium, and they'd give us presents with all these other kids. They'd give Mom food. Sam and me, we knew. Even when we were real little, we knew it was bad. Charity bad."

"You were close to your brother."

"We're like brothers, Sam and me."

137

"Did he mention he was planning something like this?"

"What exactly is this? I heard murder. You said maybe forty people, but no one's really told me. What exactly happened?"

They stared at one another, but Nick spoke first.

"Can I go to the bathroom?"

⚬≈⚬

Such clarity, Nick thought in the bathroom as he splashed water on his face. Very clear thinking here in that room with the police asking me questions. About murder. All disasters pale. I never imagined this. Who does? Who has a family member go on a shooting spree and say, upon hearing the tragic news, 'Ah, geez, I knew it. I knew it would be Bob. Everyone said it would be Gus, but no. I knew. Well, can't say I'm surprised it's Bob.'

What was going through Sam's mind? Aside from that bullet, I mean. I can't believe I thought that. Sam killed all those people? How many people? Forty. That's a misprint. But let's say it's just ten. Just ten.

I must be going insane. He's at home watching television. It's some sort of a joke. I know this, and I'm denying that I'm going through denial because Sam's at home laughing so hard.

Questions. And more questions. Was I in on it with him? They'll lock me up. Murder. They'll charge me with counts—multiple counts. Like those nameless people from Cuba or Puerto Rico who kill lots of people by setting fires in discos.

Only Sam did it personally, with guns. Up close. Shooting. Maybe there's a growth in his brain. Maybe he was a time bomb all these years, walking around with this thing ticking, ticking and ticking. When we slept in the same room as kids, it was ticking. Driving out to Arizona from Detroit. An alarm clock waiting. Bing!

No. Sam is Sam. He's no nut. I've known the guy my whole life. Something's wrong here. They should reconsider. They should do a proper investigation. They got something wrong. My brother is no murderer, and he certainly ain't no murderer times forty. Will they charge Sam? Do they charge you if you're dead?

❧

"So, what you're saying is, Sam shot all these people," Nick said to Perry when he got back. "How many? Forty? Forty people. Then he killed himself. Forty people? And you need to find out why."

"Yes," Perry said. "I know this is difficult."

"Let's do it, then," Nick said. "Enough messing around. Let's get to it. Anything I can do. If this is important, I want to help."

"Great."

"At the end of this, you'll know Sammy didn't do this," Nick said. "You guys made some kind of mistake. But, hey, that's okay. We'll clear it up."

"Sure."

"Forty people. No way. Sam, he gets teary and bent out of shape if some dog is hurt. He'd be in mourning for a week if he hit a bird or a rabbit on the road. The way he was with Moreover. He saved that dog, saved him from that asshole trying to poison him."

"Okay."

"Want to know how that happened? This guy in the neighborhood puts rat poison in meat. Meat he cooked. He took the time to cook it. Sam, he took that dog, I'll never forget, took him to the vet and nursed him back. Then he finds the the guy and tells him he does that again he'll....."

"He'll?"

"Kill him. It's an expression. Like, 'So's your mother.' Anyway, Moreover turns out to be the best dog in the world. And I don't even like dogs. Am I getting out of here soon? Because if not, can you have someone check on Moreover?"

"I'll look into that," Perry said. "You want anything? More coffee? Anything?"

"Coffee. And a cigarette would be nice. I'm out. Not menthol. I hate menthol."

❧

A regular guy. The guy's a regular guy, Perry thought in the hallway. Regular guys. Maybe that's all these two guys are. Jamokes. Slobs. Hard-working boys from Detroit. One of them shot a bunch of people to death. So what? The world's messed up. Accept it, move on. Aside from today's activity, we haven't even found a parking ticket on Sam F. Tryor.

There's a cliché. You run a name, and if he's not a killer, you say, Not so much as a parking ticket. But no one is that clean, really. We're getting nothing. Just a guy with a dog named Moreover. What kind of name is that? The Bible. Moreover, the dog. I get it. It's just not funny. I have to check on that dog. Mental note: Check on the dog. Moreover the dog.

(Could it be I was a regular guy? If so, what did that mean?)

❧

Perry headed back to the dispatch room. When he got there he leaned against the wall and looked down at his shoes, then at the carpet. He wracked his brain. There was something he was missing. He thought I seemed like a nice enough guy. Except for killing all those people, of course. He thought he would have probably shot a game of pool with me.

"Hey, Walt," Bev said. "How's our boy in there? Is he spilling his guts?"

"Not yet, Bev," Perry said. "But it's okay. How's it hanging out here?"

"We're surrounded."

"Yeah," Perry said, with no idea what she was talking about

"No, Walt, really. The station is surrounded."

"Surrounded? By who?"

"Reporters. There's about seventy of them out there. And they say they're not leaving. They elected a representative, and they're going to send him in. They have demands. There's also about two hundred other people out there. Demanding police action."

"You're serious."

"Dead. We can't leave. My shift was over an hour ago. I'm stuck. This is like that movie. That Paul Newman movie. What was that one?"

"I don't know."

"Ralph, what was that movie?" Bev said to Cortez, who was coming down the hall. "That Paul Newman movie where the police station gets surrounded like ours is surrounded now?"

"*Fort Apache, The Bronx.*"

"That's the one. You sure know your cop movies there, Ralph."

"Where's the chief?" Perry asked.

"In his office," Cortez said. "He's working on how to negotiate with the media representative. I hear they're going to send Brian Williams in."

"I like him the best out of all them," Bev said.

"I think they ought to shoot them," Cortez said. "Reporters. All high and mighty. We're better off without them. I don't care if it is Brian Williams. Who the hell is he, anyway?"

141

"Ralph, take my guy some coffee. I have to talk to the chief. And, Ralph, don't talk to the suspect. Not a word. You understand?"

"Sure. Black?"

"Excuse me?"

"His coffee. How does he want it?"

"Milk. Two sugars. Hot. Don't talk to him, Ralph. If you do, I'll throw you to those reporters. I swear to God, three seconds out there they'll be sucking on your eyeballs like after-dinner mints. And bring him a cigarette. Not menthol. He hates menthol."

Perry walked to the chief's office and felt an odd, unnatural isolation. It was like he was in an airport at three a.m., or a coffee shop with that milky blue lighting at four on a winter's afternoon, or in a grammar school on a Saturday.

We're surrounded, he thought. I don't think surrounded in a good way. Although it could be we'll walk out to applause. Everyone will be grateful and happy at the great job we did on this most difficult and gruesome case. Yeah, sure. Or there could be a bunch of people in a collective mood to blowtorch us, to descend and rend from our bones our flesh because there are too many people dead at the hands of a regular guy.

❧

"What's a better way to say it, *capitulate* or *give in*?" Chief Samson pecked at his keyboard with two fingers. He peered over his glasses with his tongue stuck out. It was obvious the typing took every ounce of his concentration.

Perry considered the chief's bushy head of white hair and his mustache. He tried to think of the famous person the chief looked like.

"What's the context?" Perry said.

"The context is, 'We won't give in to you mother-fuckers nohow, no day, no way.'"

"I'd go with *capitulate*," Perry said. "It makes us sound like we're dealing from a position of strength. Which we are, right?"

"That depends. I hear Katie Couric is going to come in to talk to me. I'd like to meet her. I used to be a Dan Rather man, but Katie's got some gams."

"Dan Rather is very weird," Perry said. "Courage."

"That's what I liked about him, his oddness. His skewed sensibilities. How do you spell *capitulate*?"

"We're surrounded, you know."

"Yup. We'll have to come out with our hands up pretty soon."

"We will?"

"That was a joke," the chief said, without a smile. "I'll deal with the press."

"They're called the media. Not everyone has a press anymore."

"There's regular people mad out there, too."

"Those other people, they're fine," Perry said. "They're confused. They're not your typical, bad-ass, let's surround a police station-type people. They're having a rough time of it. Guy walks in and shoots up the local pizza joint. No rhyme. No reason. They need to know what the hell is happening. Is the world failing them, and so forth. They're the community, for God sakes."

"You have such a big heart, Walter."

"C-A-P-I-T-U-L-A-T-E."

"Thanks. Tomorrow afternoon, task force meeting," the chief said. "You have to be there. In your hand, hold a motive for this shooting. Then we do the news conference."

"Teddy Roosevelt," Perry said.

That was it!

"What about him?" the chief said.

"That's who you look like. Do you ever get that?"

"I get that. I also get the guy from the Monopoly game. You have to do the news conference, Walter. We have no choice, here. We need to give out some answers. Maybe you can mimeograph something up beforehand for a presentation. There'll be the media—all of it—the fort, the city, a parent's group, some politicians."

"Fuck. Fuck fuck fuck."

"You sound like you're behind the wheel, Walter. So, what answers are we going to give these fine folks? What, besides *fuck*, can you tell me?"

"Sam Tryor is still his name. He's from Detroit, originally. I've got his brother in the box. He's a nice guy. Nick Tryor."

"Nick Tryor. I know him. The guy's a millionaire."

"No shit."

"Yup."

"I didn't get that feeling," Perry said. "It doesn't look like his brother Sam was sick or crazy. Not yet, at least. An MRI on his skull was clean. It doesn't appear he was depressed. Robbery was not a motive. The guns belong to a guy named Harry Bronsky. He's in holding. On our boy, though, we haven't even got a parking ticket on Sam Tryor."

"Bullshit," the chief said. "There's not a soul breathing or dead who doesn't have at least a ticket. Gandhi once did fifty in a school zone. I'll have someone find some dirt."

"Sam was stationed at Fort Huachuca. Nick says he was a listener back in the days when Cuba and Russia were sticking it to us daily."

"Great, a spy."

"I don't think so, but if you could call someone over there and run him, we'll make sure he's not government hot."

"Done. You going to go over to this guy's place?"

"Yup. I'm almost done with Nick. Then, I was thinking I would get some sleep? Good. We'll be able to wrap this up tomorrow. I think. The reason is probably at home in his phone book or between his box spring and mattress."

"Make sure you're alone in the guy's place," the chief said. "I got cops giving interviews like it's Maria Shriver out behind the station trading hand jobs for sound bites. I already got the state and Fed guys climbing the walls, and if something unexpected or bad comes out, they're going to yank this away from us before tomorrow."

"Would you do it with Maria Shriver?"

"She's pretty scary-looking. Her face is too many triangles, and chiseled. Plus, she's married to Arnold."

"Imagine their children," Perry said. "All muscle and bone and big old jaws all jutting out. Like a Cubist painting. So, would you do her?"

"I'm hot for Barbara Walters. What can we tell CNN tonight?"

"The investigation is continuing."

"We're surrounded. That's not going to cut it. I need something solid. Like this guy was working with someone?"

"He was alone. Definitely alone. No plots, no hit men, no errors."

"The guns? Can we give them something on those?"

"Give them Mr. Harold Bronsky, twenty-two. No convictions. Call him a person of interest."

"What else? We need more, Walter."

"The shooter shot himself after his rampage. We know no amount of security could have prevented this horrible tragedy. The man gave no indication of his intentions, in writing or verbally to anyone before he went to the restaurant. That he may have been motivated to be famous is something we've not completely discounted, but we have found no indication or evidence to support that at this time."

"Anything else?" the chief said.

"Sam Tryor lived in Sierra Vista for at least thirty years. He has family in town, and they are cooperating with police. We expect no one to be charged in the shooting. An emergency autopsy is scheduled later tonight to determine whether Mr. Tryor had a medical condition that might shed light on his actions. We know that, as he opened fire, he said, 'Bad day for the home team.'"

"Not a great day for the visitors, either."

ᗒᗕ

"Hell," Cortez said bitterly to Perry before he went back in to talk to Sam.

"What's up, Ralph?"

"Ain't no Brian Williams. Ain't no Charlie Gibson. They say they're going to send us Bernard Shaw. Believe that? Guy was scared of the window in the Persian Gulf War."

"Cortez, Cortez, what a killer."

ᗒᗕ

"Did Sam own any guns?" Perry asked Nick. They were in the home stretch of the interview. Perry wanted to wrap things up formally and move on.

"Not that I know of," Nick said. "He's not a big gun guy."

"Did Sam have any enemies?" Perry slid into using "Sam" instead of "your brother." He had, by this time, moved to the third chair, the one that had been between himself and Nick.

Things seemed to be going well. They were close enough now to bitch like old ladies once in a while. Nick didn't complain about the milk in his coffee. Perry seemed to enjoy the back-and-forth, the mental nudging that can happen in a good interview.

"Enemies?" Nick said. "None that I know of. No."

"Did he have any girlfriends?"

"He was going out with Dottie, but they broke that off a few months ago. She's an idiot anyway."

"So, Dottie...what's her last name?"

"Supre. Dottie Supre."

"Dottie was an idiot, and his ex-wife was an idiot. Or...what was it? A diphthong?"

"Yeah."

"Was Sam a real smart guy?"

"Not really. Couple semesters at college. Community college. Dropped out. He read a lot. All the time, reading. Smart, though? I mean, I don't know. He's smarter than me, but that's not saying much. God, I'm tired. Sam likes to say, 'I'm not smart. The rest of the world is real stupid.' I always thought that was pretty funny."

"What was Sam's business?"

"He sold double-wides. You know, houses. He'd joke that you know you've made it when you had a double-wide in Lordsburg. That was it. But he helped a lot of people buy houses. Like Jimmy Stewart in *It's a Wonderful Life*. He started that park out on Highway Thirty-four."

"Lowly Park?"

"Lolie Park. Yes."

"Business was good?"

"Great."

"I hear you're a successful businessman yourself, Nick."

"Yeah. I'm in rock."

"'N' roll?"

I remembered how Nick loved that question. He enjoyed telling people "I'm in rock." And they'd say, thinking he was a celebrity, "Rock 'n' roll?" He loved when that happened. "No," he'd say, "just rock, no roll."

The lawyers, accountants, business managers called it *aggregate*, but to Nick it was rocks, gravel, sand, and earth—same as twenty-five years ago when he got into it. Back then, when we first came out to Arizona, it was him and two guys with shovels and picks. Soon, he got a bulldozer and a crane. The company grew like crazy.

That's because everyone uses rock. Rock is put in chicken feed and in roadways, in jet fighters, cars and Titan missiles. Every man, woman and child in America uses an average of nine pounds of aggregate every year.

That's what the people in the suits told Nick. That meant a lot of money to him. It also meant he had to spend time in office suites, talking about product placement, diversification, new market evaluations. It meant less time on-site. He loved to be on-site and feel the rock wrench free and tremble at the dynamite explosions.

In the last few years, he still went to the pit, though it wasn't much fun anymore. He still loved to watch the heavy machinery scoop up the ground. But he watched it from a distance, like it belonged to some unseen conglomerate that had gained control over him.

He was not an idea man. He was nuts-and-bolts. He was the kind of guy who did the mindless grunt work all his life, and then he got stuck with a business that ran itself. He often wondered how that happened.

When Martin Marietta made moves to buy the company, I told him to sell it off and retire. Or, I told him, he should do something completely new. I told him to get a boat and cross the Pacific. Buy a casino in Las Vegas. Go to college—hell, *buy* a college. I said he should go to some fancy men's store in New York and tell the salesman he wanted to buy what *he* was wearing, and make him hand over his clothes. With money, I told him, he could do anything.

"You could buy a Ford Fairlane, like the one we used to have," I told him once in his kitchen. "You could retrace our steps. You can see where we went wrong. You could live your life all over. Oh, this is great. Yeah. Go back to Henry Ford High and pass all your tests. You could tell old Mrs. Freidkin to fuck off if she caught you smoking. It'll be fun. I'll do it with you."

～～

"No," Nick said to Perry. "No roll. Just rocks. I sell rocks. Got another cigarette?"

"Was Sam seeing a doctor for medical, or any other, problems?"

"No. He's healthy as a horse. Strong. Sam's very strong. He's such a strong man. Can I have a moment?"

Perry looked at his piece of paper on the clipboard and crossed off some more of the motives he had listed: Suicide, depression, business problems, psycho, bad relationship, media superstar, robbery gone bad, government experiment gone bad, in deep trouble, desperate.

They had been going at it for three hours. Perry had nothing. He decided to try another way.

"Nick," he said, "do you know what a black box is?"

"On airplanes. The things they always go right to after a crash."

"Right."

"They're not really black, you know," Nick said. "I saw one once. They're orange. I guess black sounds better, though."

"Do you know why they have them?"

"To find out what causes the crash."

"Exactly. Because people want to know."

"Of course, they do."

"They want to know what causes the crash," Perry said. "Was it human error? Was it mechanical? But you know what else they want to know?"

"This is going to be bad, isn't it?"

"No, it's going to be all right. They want to know about the impact. They want the screams. They want to hear the people in the plane as it hits the ground at three hundred miles per hour. They need to know about the moment of impact. Like that Capa photograph of the Spanish-American War."

"That man jerking his head when he was shot. I've seen that."

"It's the moment of death," Perry said. "From that, someone can make a computer-generated diagram out of it. They can pinpoint where everyone was standing at each second of the event. That way we can all try to understand what no one but the dead can tell us."

"That's what we're doing," Nick said, still trying to be helpful. "They don't have black boxes in restaurants. So, we've been doing this."

"We need the voices, Nick. We need Sam's voice. The space shuttle crew, remember that? Were they alive after the explosion? What were they saying? Did they know? What was going through their minds before they hit? What will go through ours?"

"Did they know?"

"We need to have our black boxes," Perry said. "We usually get them. Ten years after the Challenger explosion and *Sixty Minutes* is asking Christa MacAuliff's parents what was going though their minds as they watched their daughter die. We make movies about September eleven, trying to make sense of it. We imagine what was said by the passengers when the planes hit the buildings."

"They're out there making black boxes of today, aren't they?"

"Yes."

"I'm wracking my brain. I don't know why he did it. Do you?"

"No," Perry said. "We might never know. We never heard the real black boxes from the Challenger. But, I don't want any interview on *Sixty Minutes* ten years from now. I want to give them a black box from that restaurant soon."

"Sam had this habit, from quitting drinking. To calm himself down when he wanted a drink, he would say to himself exactly what he was doing. It's an AA thing, I think."

"He would say what he's doing?"

"Yes," Nick said. "For instance, 'I'm talking to Detective Walter Perry about a shooting today. I am sitting in a metal chair, and I am looking at Detective Perry, and I am saying I am talking to Detective Perry.'"

"Uh-huh."

"It calms Sam down. He does it all the time. I don't know. It's something, right?"

"Good. That's good. We want more of that. But, first, you sleep on all this. Let me know. It's been a long day."

"Thanks. Anything else you need? From me? I mean, about Sam."

"Yes, actually. What kind of driver was Sam?"

"You mean, in a car?"

"Yup."

"He was careful. He'd be real slow pulling out into traffic. He never tailgated. I don't know. But it goes back to the apologizing thing, sort of. He expected people to cause accidents, and he was always braced for it. He didn't trust them. It's like 'I'm not smart, the world is stupid.' It's all tied up. I don't know. Really. I can't think anymore."

"All right, Nick. It's okay. I'll take you home. Or to your car, whatever you like."

"And Moreover? You'll check on him?" Nick said.

"Sure," Perry said. "You have my word."

∽☙

I was a good person. I owned a dog and a business. People liked me. Even the detective investigating my murderous rampage seemed to like me. My brother and I were close. It came as a relief. That narrowed down the possibilities about why I did it. I had snapped. Now I just had to find out what made me I snap.

—10—

*P*erry sat in his car and reviewed what he knew. The chief wanted this wrapped up by tomorrow. And I want to pitch in the next World Series, Perry thought.

There wasn't any suspect other than me. Perry had the cooperation of the family. I have got to get that dog, he thought. Moreover. First thing in the morning.

He had access, and he didn't have to worry about a murderer on the loose. It wasn't like I would kill again if he didn't catch me. All he had to do was figure out why I walked into the Pizza Man and, after eating one slice and starting another, got up, pulled out an AK-47 belonging to another person and started shooting the other patrons.

Before he started his car, he took a moment and sat in the quiet. It was one-thirty a.m. It was quiet everywhere in Sierra Vista. It was the kind of town where they rolled up the sidewalks before midnight. Primetime TV ended at ten o'clock, and they didn't even have daylight saving time in Arizona. Perry let out an end-of-the-day sigh.

It could be he didn't like them, so he shot them, Perry thought. Could it be that simple?

Could it? I wondered.

The Cadillac started as smoothly as usual. Its power flooded into Perry's pores. He had an active imaginary life. He played his little game.

It's an eleven-minute ride, on average, he thought. My longest time was thirty-two minutes. My record is five-point-nine.

— *Can he break his own record? That's what we're all asking today.*

In addition to Walter Winchell, Perry also had a sinusy sportscaster-guy voice in his head. He was a silver-haired man named Stu, who spoke to a color commentator named Chris, who sat with him high in the stands and wore a wide tie with a large knot.

Maybe Sam Tryor thought he was in a movie. Like he was in the middle of Russian agents out to kill him because of cannoli. Like The Manchurian Candidate. *Sinatra. What the fuck is that song?*

— *Walter Perry set his record of five-point-nine minutes seven months ago,* Stu said. *Clear night. No breeze.*

Maybe Sam was rational. More than rational. Maybe his shooting was, to him, an act of benevolence.

It was a hell of a clear night, that record-setting night. Perry rolled in his car so fast and so sure, and there was nothing in his head but the ride in front of him the whole time. It was like what they say about playing golf, that there's no room for anything but that white ball.

— *Haven't you ever wanted to shoot a restaurant full of people, Chris?* Stu said.

— *Interesting question, Stu. Perry looks ready for that record tonight. Time of night—perfect. Nothing moving but the sun on the other side of the world. Conditions painfully clear. An immaculate night, ripe for the conception of a new best time home. He's looking very steady. No problems with the machinery. It's humming perfectly, and we're almost set to go, here. And I never wanted to kill anyone in my life, except for my bitch ex-wife, Stu.*

Perry edged the car to the lip of the smiling road. He gripped the steering wheel; he kneaded it in his fists like he was trying to wring something more out of it to get him home as fast as possible. He slipped the gear into neutral and gunned it. The car swayed side-to-side from the power.

— *And it sure looks like we're ready, Chris.*

Perry held his watch in front of his face to get his exact start time. He focused his eyes on the second hand because this one was for the record. *What did they do with Sam Tryor's truck? Is it in the parking lot? I'll check on it tomorrow.*

He looked at the dash and ran his hand along the steering wheel. He thought about the day he'd traded in his Pontiac and lost his pride to get this car. And I went along for the ride.

෧෨

"A Pontiac Firebird, now, there's a car," the car dealer said the day Perry drove onto the lot. Perry got out of his Firebird like he was shaking off a second-hand bad habit.

"I'd like to see the seventy-three Eldorado on the corner, there," he said.

"That's a sweet one," the dealer said. "Biggest—"

"I know all about that car."

"Yes. Well, a big fellow like yourself needs a big car. Anyway," the dealer said to Perry. "That's a nice car, that one. But we have some newer models you should look at. Now, I know they look small, but it's the interior, you see."

The man wasted his time walking around that lot with Perry for forty-five minutes. Perry let him because he wanted to be nice, and one way to be nice was to let people think they were earning their money. So, he

nodded and appeared mystified by the clever engineering improvements, how the smaller engines provided as much power as the big ones. But, he wanted
that white 1973 Cadillac. Not some new, tiny toy car.
He wanted an old piece of Detroit steel with some
kick, some flash. He wanted one like you see all the
frail, poor-sighted Arizona retirees driving around in
with their handicapped plates, bad attitudes, knobby
knuckles and AAA stickers. A '73, like the one he'd had
back in Baltimore.

"So? What do you say, big fella. Still thinking you
want the Eldo?"

Called it an "Eldo." Christ, Perry thought.

"How much trade-in on the Pontiac?" he asked.

They walked over to Perry's car, the dealer looking
at it, humming in consideration with that tilt-headed
posture the way a plumber looks at a set of pipes.

"I'll write a figure down here."

"Don't write any figures. It's got a bluebook of
twenty-five hundred. I'll give you my car and a thousand dollars. You give me six months unlimited mileage
warranty, I drive it off now."

"Four months, three thousand miles."

"Done."

Perry, for the first time since he'd been on that lot,
smiled for real.

The man went into the dealership office and yelled
to Perry, who stayed outside looking at the car. The
dealer, who was about Perry's age—46—was going on
about cars and how things used to be and about how
everything sucks now. Perry half-listened to the time-
killing chatter. Then the dealer made a call to someone
else, and Perry heard the man's muffled voice say the
word.

"Pontiac. You know what they say that stands for:
Poor Old Nigger Thinks It's A Cadillac. Heh-heh. Je-

sus. How's about you double that, and we're good to go."

Nigger.

Perry had heard the word before, of course. It had been a long time since he'd heard it, though. Anger, shock, hatred from that word. It was building, growing in Perry so that he thought he'd see it happening if he looked, that he'd be like a cartoon character expanding with water at the end of a hose.

Nigger.

I cannot believe it, Perry thought. Arizona. Arizona is what it is. These people. They have no sense, no soul here. Nothing. It's all baked out of them or something. Drive-thru liquor stores and legal guns. Chain gangs. Martin Luther King Day. No daylight saving.

"Excuse me?" Perry yelled.

The dealer looked up from his call and stopped all movement when his eyes met Perry's.

"I got to go, Frank," he said.

"You know," the dealer said, walking out of his office with the paperwork, "It's a saying's all. Something people say."

"People do say things like that."

Don't have to take this from a guy like that, Perry thought. No one should take this. Even if I do vote Republican now. Then again, I wish I could flip a switch. Calm down.

He had seriously researched the car in the man's lot. He was that kind of guy. He ran the plates on it, found the original owner, a nice woman who never drove over forty-five miles an hour in her adult life. The thing had no rust. Forty-three thousand miles.

*I'm not going to get a deal like this again. But...*nig-ger?

Perry folded his arms.

"Well, now," the dealer said, struggling to act natural but bracing to have the sale slip away, "we're all set here. You give me your keys and a check, and that baby's all yours."

But *nigger*. Nigger? That's a bad word. Like *cunt*. It sounded bad. It was a blunt-edged, hateful, hurtful, damaging, raw, mean word. *Nigger*.

The dealer stood studying Perry's face, looking doubtful that he wouldn't get a beating from this large black man, and nodding in apology. Perry unfolded his arms slowly, reached into his pocket, took out his car keys and his wallet, which he let drop open so his badge hung large, shiny and dreadful in front of the dealer.

"If there's any problem with this car," he said, "I'm bringing it back, and I expect you to fix it."

A weak threat. Driving off the lot that day, he invented stronger threats while replaying how he would have preferred that scene to go. Even years later, idling at traffic lights, he would return to that dealer and make it into a moment of racial glory. He imagined how he lectured the dealer, hit the dealer, arrested the dealer, slapped the dealer, killed the dealer or—the best to him—ran the dealer over with his Cadillac, the car to which he belonged more than it belonged to him.

— His concentration seems to have been momentarily broken here, Chris. Wonder what's on his mind?

I've got to get better voices in my head, Perry thought. These guys kind of suck.

He gunned the car onto Fry Boulevard, and thought how wonderful it was when night and desolation came together like it did just then. He turned the wheel and swung the Cadillac around. The weight slipped in an arc perfectly and settled into the lane with what seemed like a click.

It's open. Open all night. And I'm a child, and this is my car and I love it. This is me here. Pump the gas. Slowly press the accelerator down; like a trigger, you squeeze.

Under the weight of his foot, the speedometer needle bounced up to fifty. He reached the first plateau. After a few seconds, the speed yielded to Perry's adjusted sensibilities. The stoplights and the telephone poles and the intersections didn't really zip by. It was more like they lumbered and strolled past his car.

Now faster, but slowly. So I can feel the slight curvature of the earth. I'm not going to hit a light.

— *He's not going to be seeing reds, and you need that, Chris.*

Sleep, everyone. Sleep and stay at home. Allow me to drive through this grid-patterned town.

The car and Perry hit seventy. It surprised him because he knew to look down every five miles per hour or so.

Damn. Yes. My street ought to be coming up pretty soon here. I should keep going. Forever. Forever. Let's hit eighty.

He pressed his foot to the floor, and the lights, the lines, the lull, the Jack In The Box, the record store, the school, the lingerie shop, Grady Beauregard's Dodge-Chrysler-Jeep, the oil change and nail-and-hair and barber and pet grooming and sports cards collecting and Yu-Win Chinese take-out, the Exxon and 76 and Shell and Texaco and military hardware and gun and fish-and-tackle and sporting goods and Burger King and bowling lanes and Smuggler's Inn and Cloud 9 Motel and Holiday Inn and shoe stores and Walmart and movie theater and, finally, the Pizza Man became crushed into a fat, meaningless blur.

It's like, Perry thought, in the movies, when a spaceship is punched into hyperspace, and the stars become a flattened and insignificant backdrop. It is a night for doing what has not been done before, of records, of forty dead, of a matter of minutes to home, of clarity and control and excess, the sickness of the day draining out like an infection of the soul compressed and healed by sleep and God smiling and the earth opening forty cold holes to receive them. Forty-one when you count Sam Tryor.

He hit his watch. Five-point-seven minutes. It was a new record. And the crowd went crazy.

Perry walked into his house and laid his gun on the kitchen table. His wife stared at the .357 with wide eyes. She always kept an eye on the gun. She never mentioned how bizarre she regarded the gun, or how it trembled the center of her stomach. She couldn't mention it.

"Hi," Winsome said before she let her eyes get back to polishing her nails.

That was Perry's wife's name. Winsome. As in charming, winning.

"What have you—"

"Get me a napkin," she said when a glop of nail polish ran down her finger. It looked like a blob of knife-drawn blood. "Thanks. What were you saying?"

"Nothing," Perry sat down at the table. "What you doing?"

"Curing cancer. You?"

"Figuring out why some guy shot forty people."

"I heard about that. They put that on you, huh?"

"I spoke to the guy's brother today. Regular guy. Normal."

"The brother?"

"Both of them. Both normal, regular guys."

"What did you expect?"

"I don't know. A profile fitter. A sicko. Junkie, terrorist, kid, guy fired from his job, guy who lost his wife, robbery gone bad, like that."

"I see," Winsome blew on her nails and closed the bottle of nail polish with her fingers tensed and spread like she was handling uranium. "You're expecting if you saw the guy on the street before he did this, you would stop and arrest him for suspicion of mass murder."

"Thus singlehandedly preventing the deaths of many innocent people."

"Remember...oh, what's his name? Weather?"

"The Weathermen? They were killers all right. They—"

"No. Shut up for a second."

They sat in silence. Winsome thought and stared at gun on the table. Perry waited, curious about what she was thinking. Then the silence grew, and it seemed like Winsome's idea, whatever it was, was going to vanish like smoke from a fire that didn't get going.

"Starkweather!" she said. "Charles Starkweather! Remember, in Nebraska? He shot all those people for no reason. Like him."

"Charles Starkweather was a nut."

"Maybe the guy today was a nut. Mrs. Lopez, across the street, she thinks her son was in that restaurant. You know, Carlos? Her youngest. I came home from work, and she stopped me to say he's been missing since early today and could you check to make sure."

"Carlos is a drug dealer," Perry said. "He's missing because that's what he does. He's a professional stay-away-from-home-type person."

"Still, you never know."

"I'm glad you waited up."

"You think those people got shot today because they deserved it?" Winsome asked. "I mean, I didn't wait up for you. I had a date."

"I figured you did, but I was trying," Perry said as the weight of the day pressed in on him. We need answers, he thought. Why. Why do we need to know why?

"No one deserves to be shot while eating pizza," he said. "We should get some sleep."

"I didn't like the guy I went out with," Winsome said. "All he talked about was the shooting today. That's all everyone was talking about at the Village Inn. Some kids were laughing about it and making believe like they were shooting and getting shot. It was weird. I guess they'll be talking about it for a while."

"I'll see you in the morning," Perry said. He got up, put his hand tenderly around his wife's upper arm and squeezed in an attempt to reassure her.

Winsome gripped Perry's hand and smeared one of her freshly painted nails. She stared straight ahead.

"People shouldn't kill other people, Walter," she said. "They shoot everyone in the movies and on television, and for pretend during dinner in this little town. It bothers me. You've been shot. I bet it feels awful. Those people knowing there was nothing they could do in that restaurant. Nothing but get shot or maybe not get shot today. That man. Killing. How horrible."

They both looked dead tired, worried and like they were wondering about everything all at once. Then they went to sleep, saddened, but together in one bed for the first time in a long time.

⟨≈⟩

Nick drove his Cadillac home, but without Perry's drama. After all, he was only driving a Catera. Perry had driven Nick to where he'd left it, just a few blocks from the Pizza Man. Nick got into his car and handed Perry my house key. He reminded him about Moreover and almost ended up weeping about the dog, the safety and care of that dog.

I'm not a smart man, Nick thought as he drove. I wish I was. Seems like ten years since I've been in this car. Today has lasted forever, and I can't bear to think any longer. Sam, I wish we could talk about this. Jesus, you're dead. You were so good and knowing about people. You would know why this happened.

Nick drove home on autopilot. If he were ever asked, he wouldn't remember anything about making the trip. He looked up and saw John's Ice Cream. It was where he and I would go and get the flavor of the month every month and celebrate nothing in particular. Nick thought about the last time we were there.

The memory of that day at John's Ice Cream came back to Nick, and back to me when it did.

We sat outside, Nick thought. That family. The things he said about that family. Hold it. Think about this stuff later. Don't think about this now. *I have to save this. Hold it for later. Think about it at home.*

We sat outside, and it was sunny that day. It was the first of May.

Nick stopped thinking about it, but I knew it would come back later.

Three miles slipped by. Nick lit a cigarette, the last in the pack. I should stop for another pack, he thought. I have a pack at home. Somewhere, I'm sure. Almost home now.

He got home and sat in his car in the driveway. He just sat there and let himself feel tired. The momentum of driving was still with him.

Nick walked to his door and sensed something was off. It was like his yard and his house weren't how he'd left them. Did you ever get the feeling that, while you were away, someone came in and replaced everything with exact replicas? Nick recalled how an annoying kid from high school said things like that. Lou Gehrig gets Lou Gehrig's disease. What are the odds? That was another one.

There was a scrawled note stuck between the screen door and the front door of Nick's house: WE DON'T WANT THE MURDERERS HERE GO BACK HOME. Nick looked behind him. He expected the neighbors to be standing there carrying torches. But they weren't. They were asleep.

Once inside, he looked at his answering machine. Is there someone here? he thought.

The machine light flashed with messages. He looked around and had the feeling it was someone else's house and he was intruding.

"Hey," Nick yelled. "Hey. Go away. I'm home and you can get out now." Silence. "Gosh, I sure sound tough."

He sat on his couch. He reached over and hit play on his machine.

Beep. "Mr. Tryor? This is Mike Flahgg. Channel Eight. I know this is difficult, but if you could, call me at five-five-five-two-nine-eight-seven when you get a chance. Or page me at five-five-five-eight-six-five-five. I want to talk to you about your brother and what happened today. Thanks. And if there's anything I can do for you, let me know."

Beep. "Mr. Tryor, Gwen Pelicran, with the *Daily Star*. If you're home, can you pick up? Hello? I hope this is the right number. I'll try back later."

Beep. "Nicky, it's Dottie. I heard about Sammy. Unreal. Such a shame. I'm in shock. Shock. I wanted to tell you, all these reporters have been calling. They say...well, they want to talk to me. I don't know what to tell them. And you. They asked to talk to me with you. I said I'd ask if you wanted to be together, so we can tell them about Sammy. Together. Give me a call."

Beep. "You're next, you piece a shit. That's right. I'm coming for you. Be real careful—"

Nick turned down the volume so the messages would play out and he didn't have to hear them. I am so bored with shootings and death and killing and questions and motives and reasons, he thought. Why did he do it? I don't know. I wish I knew, but I don't.

◞✦◟

"The world has gone to hell ever since they put nipples on mannequins," I said to Nick that day at John's Ice Cream. He remembered and thought about it as he sat on his couch and his messages played so he couldn't hear them.

"Well, they made John's Ice Cream, so it's not so bad," Nick said. He swung his leg over a tiny stool that was attached to a tiny table outside, then sat down.

We watched four people come out of John's. They looked up at the overcast Arizona afternoon and decided to sit down at a one of the other small metal tables.

"I'm serious," I said. "Why put nipples on mannequins? What's the point?"

"That's funny. I get it. 'What's the point.'"

"I wasn't making a joke. I don't know, Nick. It's sad. People."

"You've been doing this since you were in the second grade," Nick said, pointing at me with his mocha-caramel cone. "You're always preaching doom-and-gloom. Give it a rest. Things are good. Life is good. People are good. Maybe not as good as you would like, but still—good.

"Everyone's always going on about how terrible things are. Everyone's bad and dumb, and kids today blah blah blah. Enough. Maybe all that talking is what makes things so terrible. Ever think of that? Besides, you're not close enough to dying to be this depressing."

"Sure I am," I said. "We all are."

"I'm not old," Nick said. "You are not old. Fifty-two is not old. If you were to die tomorrow, everyone would go around, and they would be saying…what?"

"'How am I going to collect the money that motherfucker owes me?'"

"Okay. The second thing would be 'What a shame. He was so young.'"

"We're old. Not walking-with-an-aluminum-walker old, but old. We're from the generation that thinks it's important to have shined shoes. We're old. Checking out eighteen-year-old girls creepy old."

"Man," Nick said. "What the hell kind of bug is up your ass today?"

"Nothing."

We sat in silence.

"Mocha-caramel," Nick said. "That's a good flavor."

"Yeah."

"So, you seeing anyone new these days, or what?"

"Nah," I said. "You know, this and that."

"You're in a mood today," Nick said before he sucked hard at his ice cream. He looked up, and he caught sight of a terrible sadness in my face. It frightened him. "I know you're a vanilla man, but…"

"Look at them," I said to him. "Look at them sitting there. They have no reason in their heads."

He turned his head and saw the family. There were two young girls, a man and a woman. They were busy eating their ice cream at the table across from us. One of the girls slipped off her stool, went down to the ground and laughed.

"Sit up," the mother said, her words like a smack. The girl ignored her. "What do you think this is? What's wrong with you?"

Without looking at any member of his family, the man said, "Lisa, let her alone. She has to learn. All right?"

"I told you to sit up straight. How many times?"

The four of them seemed so lost to each other. The other girl got up and stood very still to make an important point in her ongoing protest.

"Patty, why don't you eat?"

"'Cause it sucks, that's why," the other girl said. She didn't move a muscle, she just narrowed her eyes and tightened her mouth.

"I don't know anymore," the mother said to no one.

Maybe Sam was saying something that day, Nick thought now, sitting on the couch. Maybe I should tell that cop. Maybe he'll know.

Nick said these things, but in another part of himself, he vowed never to tell anyone about that day and about the look on my face as I criticized that family of four.

That family angered me, I admit it. I don't know why, specifically; they just did. There was so much meanness and unhappiness coming off them. I couldn't figure it out. I still have no idea where that comes from in people.

"Do you ever think they're worthless," I said to Nick.

"Who?"

"People."

"No. I don't think like that. It's like what Anne Frank said. 'In spite of everything, I still believe people are good.'"

"Look what they did to her," I said.

"Damn," Nick said. "I think people *are* good. So do you, remember? We genuinely like people. Some are bad, but we believe most are okay."

"I don't know," I said. "I just don't know anymore."

"Your ice cream is melting all over your hand," Nick said, handing me a napkin. "Sometimes you think too much, Sam. That's your problem. Let's say they *are* worthless. So what? What does that have to do with you?"

"Everything."

"You think too much, Sam."

"If Van Gogh were around today, I think he'd take a few people with him before he killed himself."

Nick laughed and looked up at me. He didn't get the joke. He didn't know whether I was even making a joke. I didn't either. Nick told me he felt strange for laughing, but for some reason, he couldn't stop.

☙

Nick sat and stared. The picture of him and me in the shadows made the photo seem more there, like a person sitting in the dark next to you not saying anything.

Something big and hard hit his window. Nick went to look out. He saw a Camaro speed off and heard someone inside it yell, "Fuck you, motherfucker!"

There was a rock below the window.

His answering machine was still going. He turned it up. Some guy told him that a picture of me and him would be on the cover of *Newsweek*. He said they got it from a photo lab. Did he have a comment?

Nick dialed Perry's number and left a message about the rock.

There is probably a mob coming together outside my house. They can take me and drag me out and kill me. No big deal, Nick thought. The picture of my brother and me is going to be on the cover of *Newsweek*.

Over the next hour, Nick called Perry four times and left four messages. He sat on the couch between calls and held the photo and cried without knowing why or for what or for who.

Forty people, he thought. It's all relative, really. Forty people dead. That's a big deal. Forty people dead is not always a big deal, though. It's relative. At Auschwitz, more than four thousand people were killed per day. Yesterday, Sam did a little more than point-zero-one percent of one day at Auschwitz. That's the math.

In his last message for Perry, Nick said, "When we were young, back in Michigan, the big kids wanted to play hockey where we were playing. Sam, he said things about their mothers and army boots and stuff. The big kids couldn't pull Sam off that ice.

"He was tough, Sam was. I remember. They took their sticks and hammered through the ice and destroyed that ice so no one could use it. They wrecked it. No rules, pond hockey. That's what we played. I hope that helps. I don't know what you need."

He sat for a moment. I am nuts and bolts, he said to himself. He called a friend, woke him up, and asked if he could stay at his house in Bisbee. Of course he could, he could stay as long as he wanted.

Nick thought he might give an interview, perhaps on television, and say I was crazy. He would tell the story of John's Ice Cream. He would say I was a ticking time bomb. If he did it, it would all be over. People wouldn't hate him, they would feel sorry for him. It would be over, and he could live in Sierra Vista in peace. He would be able to sleep at night. All he had to do was go on TV for three minutes.

I thought it sounded like a good idea. I'd understand if he did it. To escape the pressure, I probably would have. I only hoped if he did become a Judas and renounce me, it would only be so he could live in peace, and not because he really believed I was crazy.

Nick stood up, showered and packed. He placed his hand on the wall by the bathroom door before he left. It was the same wall with the picture of me and him after his birthday.

He looked at the picture of us. He looked out his screen door and thought he saw eyes peering, accusing him.

As he walked to his car, Nick thought the photo would be gone when he got back—whenever that might be. He thought it would be taken as a prize, burned as a totem, hoarded like it was a splinter from the cross.

Things will change, Nick thought as he started his car. What things? Everything. Three minutes on television, and I can get my life back. I haven't felt like this since Sam and I left Detroit. Things changed then, all right. Get a Fairlane. Retrace our steps. Life changes so much in just an afternoon, in a moment. It can end, begin, begin again, change, switch, crash, rise. Life in a moment. The wall with the picture won't be there the same way when I get back. No. They'll tear it down. One way or another. No rules, pond hockey. God, he was a tough little kid.

—11—

In 1813, John Higgins was seventeen-years-old when he was killed by the mayor of Gorgon, Louisiana. Wallace Johns beat Higgins to death on a dock with a heavy iron chain when he refused to be separated from his family after he was sold at a slave auction. Johns meant the beating to serve as a warning to the other slaves.

It didn't quite work out that way. Over the years, as Higgins's family members died, they joined together and haunted Johns. They lived in his house and destroyed his furniture. Apparently, they smashed it with chains. They tipped over dishes at parties. His house clamored with the sound of clinking chains constantly, so much so that Johns couldn't be heard at his own dinner table.

He moved five times but was followed and hounded wherever he went. In the attic of the last house where he lived, thirty iron chains hung from the ceiling. They knocked together whenever a breeze blew, making a constant clinking sound, like broken bits of china falling.

After Johns died—of a stroke, in old age—his family gathered at his house for the reading of his will.

When the lawyer got to the part that said, "All of my slaves are to be divided up and sold at auction, with the proceeds going to my children," the piece of paper burst into flame. The house burned to the ground in less than thirty minutes. The lawyer and several other people escaped, but every member of Johns's family died. Afterward, they discovered the doors the family members tried to leave by had all been chained shut.

❧

The news conference was twenty minutes late starting. The crowd of reporters and people stood and rocked from foot to foot in the desert chill at eight a.m. The reporters were still wired from the day before, from all the action and information, but they were tired, too. They had run around for the last twelve hours straight, had interviewed victims in their hospital beds, checked names, checked the number of dead, rechecked and updated the stats, gotten scooped and scooped other reporters on one fact or another.

After all that, their competitive fervor was a little blunted. There was nothing to do but wait for the news conference, and then do another story on that. It was a "feeding." That's what they called it when reporters were thrown the information they needed to have for a story for the morning, five, six and noon newscasts. It was like it never stopped. A near-constant flow of information was maintained and sent out to the TV stations, then to TV sets across the country.

"I'm sorry," a woman said from the podium set up by the Sierra Vista Convention and Visitor's Bureau. It was in front of the Pizza Man so they would have a good backdrop for the news conference. "Sorry. We're running a little late. The copy machine broke, and we wanted to give you all handouts beforehand."

The reporters, the photographers, and the tech crew people ambled toward the podium.

"It's going to be a while until we can officially start," the woman said. "Before we begin, let me introduce you to Doris Lambert. She is president of the Sierra Vista Convention and Visitor's Bureau. She has something she'd like to say before we officially begin."

Doris Lambert took the floor. She was bird-thin and Nancy Reagan-fragile, more like an outline of a woman. She smiled a hollow smile and looked at the reporters. She seemed very aware she was being watched.

She tried to pick up the microphone, but it was stuck. She smiled, grimaced, frowned, then wrenched it free from the stand.

"If you'll all be patient, I want to tell you the news conference will begin shortly. We're sorry for this inconvenience, but sit tight. Thank you."

"Will there be a statement from the police?" a reporter shouted.

"Please sit tight," Doris Lambert said.

She left the podium and had an argument with a small man.

"Get your hands off!" the man yelled. Then he wrenched the microphone from Doris Lambert, who had just wrenched it free for herself. He put the mic back in its stand. He looked like he had just been rushing to or from something.

"Because we have some time, there are some people I'd like to let speak here," the man said. "My name is Bud Langston. I'm just a citizen here. Like you all. I'm not official. Although, for the record, I was, at one time, a city councilman here in Sierra Vista.

"Now, some people..." He looked at Lambert, who tightened her mouth in a frown. "...aren't too pleased with me being here, but, hey, the mic's open. There are some people who have indicated to me they want to have their say. Like I said, this isn't official or anything. So, without further ado..."

He ushered a woman up to the podium.

"My two boys were killed," she said.

Oh, God, I thought, family members. I didn't want to be there. But, like everywhere else I had been, I had no choice. I was still just along for the ride.

"Louder," a reporter yelled. "Speak up. En Inglés? I can't pick you up back here. And spell your name. We didn't get a spelling on that."

The woman at the podium stood in front of the reporters and adjusted herself to her task.

"My name is Maria Alvarez Asuelo. A-S-U-E-L-O. My two boys were killed here yesterday by the man who did this. And I am here today to ask that when they catch this man, this bad man, that he gets punished. That he gets killed, too. Am I being loud enough?"

"The guy killed himself," a reporter said.

"Yes," another said. "they caught him. He's dead and punished."

"What's the spelling of your name, again?"

"My boys Franco and Bobby were here," Maria said, bravely moving beyond her mistake. "They were eating pizza. They're in the army at Fort Huachuca. And this man came in and shot them. He came in and why? For what? You tell me. Now they are dead, and this man, this man is dead, and I say fine for his death but not fine for the deaths of Bobby and Franco. My boys. I love them so much. And now they're dead for what? No reason. No reason."

Barbara Cloven, the Hoof from the *Sierra Vista Herald*, stood close to the front of the clump of reporters. She said to another reporter, "So what?" and laughed.

But in trying to seem hardbitten, the Hoof stepped across the barrier between weathered-reporter cynicism and outright cruelty. The reporters near her, like children near a kid caught calling the teacher a bitch, went absolutely quiet. They watched Maria as she stared the Hoof down.

"So what?" Mrs. Asuelo said. "Let me tell you so what. People like this man, this killer man, should be caught before they do this sort of thing." She nodded vigorously. The reporters perked their attention toward her. "I am going to work to get the laws changed so the police can find these people. You see them on street corners. So they can be taken off the street before this happens. That's right."

"How do you plan on doing this?" Cloven asked, trying to get back in good graces.

"I am going to talk to the governor when he comes down. That's right. To see what can be done to stop these kinds of killing. These people in post offices. Restaurants. The places of work. Schools. I lost my boys. But I don't want them to have died for nothing. Maybe their deaths can lead us to find the kind of person who would do this, and stop them before they do this. Lock these types of persons up. Check them out. Keep our eyes on them."

She nodded. The reporters looked at her. Maria, who for two days after would be described by reporters as brave, determined, gutsy, incredible, amazing, a woman who refused to be a victim of senselessness, looked like she needed a big finish. She looked directly into one of the cameras.

"Anyone out there who thinks they can get away with this, who thinks they can kill good people like my Bobby and Franco. I will find you, and we will get you. I am a little woman, yes. But know that I am out there looking for you."

Maria stood and looked at the reporters and the people her speech had captivated. She held her head high. She positively beamed with adoration for herself and the courage she displayed.

Then, she broke down and wept; her shoulders heaved. No one moved toward her. No one moved away from her. Everyone heard her cry, and they diverted their eyes. They listened and stared at the ground as she struggled to gasp air between sobs. For several, awful minutes she stayed and sobbed until it was like she forgot who, and where, and what she was. It would be hours before she would be able to recall her speech.

After she was led off the platform, a guy named Len Sweet moved to the podium and straightened his bolo tie. He was up next.

He shifted his weight from one bootheel to the other. He wet his lips. He slicked his hair and slapped away his wife's hand when she reached over to slick his hair the right way. He wore a green suit made from some oil-based fabric, but he seemed comfortable in it. He looked damned proud of what he was about to say. This was his moment.

He had stacks of literature with him. He had flyers, a big banner, pamphlets, testimonials, glossy magazine ad reprints and even a stack of bumper stickers that read IF YOU BELIEVE IN GUN CONTROL RAISE YOUR RIGHT HAND that featured a drawing of Adolf Hitler gesturing as only Hitler could.

He put his hands on the podium that a moment before had dwarfed Maria Asuelo, and he shook it like it was a cardboard box. He took some time to arrange his material then gripped the podium sides tightly with his large hands and leered at the out-of-town reporters.

"What transpired to take place here yesterday," Len Sweet said into a silence brought on by the shock of his clichéd Western madman appearance, "could have been avoided. If the populace in this establishment had been armed, like the speck of pestilence who perpetrated the shooting, then that man would not have been able to load in a fresh round before he was cut decidedly and purposefully down."

Len Sweet looked out, nodded to emphasize his words then continued.

"But a bill in Congress that hinders the God-given right of free Americans to bear arms has brought on this sick, unnecessary, horrible, pathetic travesty of the human spirit.

"Others will tell you that some unfortunates *were* bearing arms at the time of this internalized conflagration. Indeed. Don't let those statements dissuade you from the reality of the future situation. If we do not alter the publication of these laws by the United States Congress, then we have all squandered a safer society for the sake of some potential politician's expedience.

"Remember to vote with your feet in this critical matter. We grieve for those whose lives are gone from us, but we'll cry even harder for lives not lived because of the freedoms we lost to a Congress unrepresentative of the majority of Americans' opinions. I have material available for you to read and photograph on the freedom-to-bear-arms issue. Thank you."

Another man stepped up and took the mic.

"Here's what it's all about," the voice on the stage boomed out. People jerked their heads around to look at him. I was transfixed. "This should not happen. Not in this community. Not in any community. And so we find ourselves asking, What happened here? Our brothers and sisters, dead or shot, while they are enjoying their holiday meal. And why? we ask ourselves."

The Rev. Marcus T. Lowell was joined on the rickety platform by eight children ranging in age from three to eighteen. They held what looked like decorative tin plates, maybe even panning tins, the kind prospectors used. They shook them in the sun occasionally as Lowell spoke, and generated stabs of light that blinded people standing in the wrong spot at the wrong time. When the reverend paused, the children looked nowhere near anyone's eyes in the crowd. They had that bored, heard-it-all-before look children have when they've heard it all before.

Rev. Lowell peered out over the crowd of reporters in accusation. He allowed his silence to linger.

"We will be told by the police they are doing all that can be done," Lowell continued. "All that can be done. We will be told how this man, this Samuel Tryor, bought his gun legally. Because buying a gun in Arizona, it's not a crime. We will be told there are many explanations for this man's actions.

"We will certainly be given many, many reasons for this. From crack babies to gang warfare, from the profit motive to the criminal motive. From a broken home to a broken heart. And it's all true. But there is no reason. *No reason.* There isn't a single reason for the deaths of these fine people here. A sick man has spread his sickness, and now it is loose like a virus upon the clean streets. It is up to us, however, to cleanse ourselves of this sickness so it does not spread."

He paused, and actually mopped his brow.

"We shall do this with love, with understanding, with kindness," Reverend Lowell said. "As they say in the old language, 'We shall go forth from this place. This now holy place.' Yes. I see you all shaking your heads. I see how you've stopped writing in your little pads, there. You'll put this on the news tonight. About how this place was a killing field.

"But on that news tonight, you won't show me calling it holy. Because that makes people scared. Yes. Frightens them something terrible, more even than the death that came to this place. Ask yourselves why that is, and you will know why this happened here today. You will know where the killer comes from. Thank you."

Doris Lambert stepped up from the opposite side as Lowell left.

"I apologize for the delay. I think now we are ready to start the briefing. No one from the police department is available right now," she announced apprehensively, sounding afraid the town had failed to provide an adequate news conference. "I should tell you that the restaurant will be cleaned later today. Tonight. I think we can get you in. Or not.

"There will be three funerals tomorrow at Green Lawn Cemetery. That will be early. The police will release preliminary autopsy results on the suspect. Later today for that. They will also answer any of your questions. That will take place tomorrow morning. What else?

"We have pictures available of the suspect. Of Sam Tryor. You can get those at the Sierra Vista Convention and Visitor's Bureau in about three hours, I'm told. Okay. Thank you all, so much. Thank you. If you have any questions, I'm available."

◦═◦

The people at the news conference were weird and mean, and that made the news conference bizarre and strange. But it was liberating for me. After it ended, I felt better. I wasn't as ashamed about what I had done. I didn't realize it until later, but that was when I began to understand why I had done what I did. That's when things started to make sense.

—12—

*T*he house where I was born, in Pottstown, Pennsylvania, was built before the Revolutionary War and was haunted by a British spy named Nelson Nottingham. When the locals came to arrest Nottingham for being a spy, he hanged himself from a beam in the living room.

The ghost did annoying things. There was a pewter cup that floated from room to room. Once, my father took the cup to Philadelphia and threw it away. The next morning, it was back in the cupboard in the kitchen.

My aunt stayed with us for a night and slept in the attic. After she heard horses on the roof and voices talking, she left and never came back.

Something bad happened to everyone who lived there, either in the house or nearby. In 1956, a man killed his wife and himself in the upstairs bedroom. In 1874, a child fell down the well out back and drowned. My mother was in a terrible car accident and almost killed less than a quarter of a mile from the house. After that, my parents moved to Detroit to be near her family so they could take care of me, my brother and my mother. Then there was me. I grew up and murdered forty people.

I became a ghost, but I didn't haunt a place. My restless spirit haunted people. Haunting just a house would have been so much easier. Either way, I knew my haunting days were coming to an end. I was getting close. It wouldn't be long before I would go away forever.

☜

"Murder, murder, murder. Death, death. Deathly, murdery death. Dead, deadly, murdery, deadly death. Make that money pay. Murder, murder, murder. Death, death."

It was a song. Winsome sang it while she buttered the waffles, smelled the coffee and cooked. Like many people who spend a lot of time alone, she was singing out loud without realizing it. She shut the refrigerator after getting the milk for the coffee and dragged her slippered foot along the linoleum and sang.

"Hmmm, deadly, death, murder, murder, murder, death, death."

It had a 3/2 beat with a change-up. She was good at jazz.

Perry could have said, "Please, honey, don't sing that song." He could have been mad, but he knew that wouldn't have helped anything.

They woke up together. They'd spent the whole night together. Last night, they'd walked to the bedroom hand-in-hand. She led him. They undressed slowly, and Perry stole glances at her body. She looked at him when he wasn't looking. They checked each other out in the low light by the bedside and then fell asleep in minutes.

After a few hours, they were together, snorting and smacking limbs, all entwined with their arms twisted around legs, around necks, around wrists, around waists, across backs. The blanket got tangled and

stretched, practically ripped in two from the force of
how they shared. Together.

When they woke up, they realized where they were
and who they were with. It felt like late on a summer
morning when actually it was six a.m., and there was a
lot to be done. They wanted to stay in bed longer because they felt perfect. Even the air and the clouds felt
perfect. The barometric pressure against their bodies.
Perfect.

"Do you think you'll catch the guy who did it?"
Winsome asked Perry in the kitchen as he chased a
glob of syrup around with his last bit of Eggo.

"They did," he said. "I told you. He killed himself.
At the scene."

"Does that mean the police caught him? Do you
count that as caught?"

"Maybe not. He caught himself. He's a self-catcher.
That's how we'll record it in that big book in the basement."

"Make fun. What else has to be done? I mean, if
he's the guy, and he's not out hurting children at play-
grounds or whatever, on account he shot himself, what
else do you do?"

"We find out why he did it."

"Why?"

"We need to know. Was the guy nuts? Were there
others involved? Was it part of something larger? Like
that."

"Why?"

"Because that's what we do. That's a big part of it,
the why."

"How long does why take to find out?"

"In this case, by four this afternoon."

"How do you find out why?"

"I go to the guy's house, and I go through all his
belongings and look for a diary entry that says, 'Mon-

day: get pizza, shoot many people. Don't forget dry cleaning.' If that happens, I tell Chief Samson, and he tells the reporters, and they all go away, and I get to be deputy chief, and we all live happily ever after. The end."

"If that doesn't happen?"

"I'll make something up."

Winsome went to the sink and put the dishes in. She hummed her "Murder, murder, murder, death, death" song. It drove Perry to the edge of his patience; he almost asked her to not sing. But he didn't.

"You busy tonight?" he asked instead.

"Yes, but I'll be home around eleven. I'm going to jump in the shower. And hey, if I don't see you tonight, then call me and let me know if you find out why. I really want to know."

Perry sat at the kitchen table and listened to his wife in the shower. He wondered about life—its causes, why it's so messed up, why more people don't kill more people in a rage. He noticed Winsome's keys on the table. On her key ring was a canister of Mace, a pair of plastic dice, eighteen keys and a stuffed Garfield doll.

"Chick keys," he said. "These are chick keys. What is with that? Everything but the sink is stuck on here. Women should do something about all the crap on their keys."

He laughed, but it was sad. He felt like he had been in the house too long, that the night had gone on too long. He wanted to change his clothes and wash up somewhere other than home. He thought the day would go better if he started it somewhere else. His wife was in the shower, and he was in the kitchen, and he felt like the last guest at a bad party and it was way past time to go. That's when he left.

❧

184

Perry saw the first few drops of rain hit his windshield. He ran down the list of things he had to do that day. He had to wash up, have a cup of coffee, gather his thoughts, talk to Chief Samson, go to my house, get Moreover, find out why I shot those people, look in the paper for rent ads, and be happy.

Monday: get pizza, shoot many people. Don't forget dry cleaning. Is that how the day went for me? Could it be that simple?

A Buick swerved onto Perry's lane.

"Fucker," he yelled. "You mother-pissing piece of dickshit bitchwad fuck!"

He was on Fry when that damned song from the morgue came back. He hummed the tune and sang, "Murder, murder, murder. La-la-la. Murdery death, deathly murder."

A VW Bug, two cars up, stopped suddenly at a yellow light.

"Pigface dickfooted honk-horn cow-humping trash-talking scum-slurping chink of gash-worshipping faggot-fucking shit."

The song was lodged in Perry's brain. It was going to stay there and eat his mind from the inside out if he didn't get the name of it. It was tricky because the only way to remember it was to not think about it. Traffic moved.

Things were coming back to me in bits and pieces. I remembered Ellen Barkin. I dated a woman, and we talked about movies, and there was an actress whose name I could not remember. It was on the tip of my tongue all evening. We went to bed, and in the middle of sex with her on top, while we were lost in the throes of passion, I looked up at her and said, "Ellen Barkin!" You remember the strangest things at the strangest times.

Perry tried to relax.

I am driving my car. I am changing the radio, Perry thought, listing every movement the way Nick told him I used to. I am looking out the rearview mirror. I am watching the light change. I am looking at the girl in the car behind me. I am noticing her face, and I am wondering if she has a brain in her head.

"These dicks," Perry exploded. "They don't get it. Everyone's mad. Mad being force-fed beer on television, mad they can't drink it on the job and madder still when they don't have more money to buy more when they run out. Mad. Madness. Mad motherfuckers everywhere."

Perry drove to Dunkin' Donuts. He walked in and tanked up his Thermos with black coffee. He loved his Thermos. It represented comfort, stability, and he loved the hell out of it. He got a bran muffin and a blueberry donut and told the sales girl he was practicing Zen as they spoke. She nodded, but you could tell she had no idea what he was talking about.

"Did you guys catch that guy from the restaurant yet?" she asked.

"Yes," Perry said, comfortable in his surliness. "We caught him. We got him in the interrogation room and he started getting all mad so...we shot him. I swear."

"Nice," she said. "But doesn't that, like, get you guys in trouble? Shooting people like that in the head?"

"But see, we dumped him back in the restaurant. We put the gun in his hand so it looks like he did it himself."

"Cool."

At the door, Perry said, "Who said anything about shooting him in the head?"

"No one," the girl said. "I just figured that's how you guys would do it. That's how I would."

☙❧

Perry drove toward my house. He remembered Samuel F. Tryor, 1540 E. Packer Street, Mountain View, Arizona 85792, organ donor. He thought back to yesterday, to the coppery scent of blood in the Pizza Man. Was that just yesterday?

"Bev," he said into the radio. "Bev."

"Say it right, Walt."

"Beverly."

"Come on, we're probably being taped by CNN even as we speak."

"The ears have walls."

"Do it right, Walter."

"Hell," Perry said. "Unit Oh-Oh-Twenty-Four to base. This is unit Oh-Oh-Twenty-Four to base. Over. Do you read me, base? This is Captain Jean-Luc Picard. Stardate Oh-Oh-Twenty-Four to base."

"Go ahead, Twenty-four."

"Base, get me the chief. Have him ten-twenty-four me in my unit. I'll be forty-five for sixteen minutes at the thirteen-twelve location. Then I'll be eighty-four until oh-eight-thirty. And that's a ten-four."

"You're in a mood today."

"Get him for me, it's important. Tell him I'm at Tryor's. Then I'm going dog hunting. Out."

"Over and."

⌕

This is exactly what the bad side of town looks like, Perry thought as we got closer to Lolie Park. It was the park I built. I was going home.

Perry drove slowly along the streets that were really just dirt trails. The place was a tattered neighborhood of trailers and double-wides. He leaned forward to see the numbers on the "houses" so he could find mine.

Of course, there are no numbers, Walter Winchell said in Perry's head. *In this area, they don't need numbers. This is white trash, RV heaven. In this area, everyone's on food stamps, welfare and cable television. In this area, people are druggie-thin and brittle or hugely fat and fragile. In this area, bills get thrown in the car's back seat and, if they are paid at all, paid late. Time stands quietly alone in a corner, and there is so much nothing to do that nothing gets done.*

In town, they call this area Lowly Park. They don't have numbers. Don't need them. They know one another. They know what they're doing.

Then he saw my place. Even without a number, it wasn't hard to miss. There was a small group of bored people smoking and staring at the ground in front of my double-wide. The screen door hung on by only the bottom hinge and banged occasionally against the wall. If those clues weren't enough, the fact the place was wrapped in yards of yellow plastic police tape was a dead giveaway. Although, in this place, it could have been anyone's house.

They've been here, Perry thought.

"Hey," he said as he got out of his car.

"Yeah," one guy said.

There were seven people in the group. It looked like all they ever did was stand around and stare, smoke generic cigarettes and roll their eyes at the latest lies they heard about last night. It was just a Tuesday morning with low cloud cover, and everyone looked aggravated and bored and mean.

There's no place like home, I thought.

"They been here?" Perry said.

"Yeah. They were here, all right," a kid about seventeen said. He sucked on a Marlboro and shook his head. "All over here."

"Is this Sam Tryor's place?" Perry asked.

"You a cop?"

"Yup. You?"

"I'm a kid."

"You know Tryor?"

"Know him? Shit. Grew up with him. Guy pretty much raised me."

The others grumbled and nodded.

"What can you tell me about him?"

The kid looked Perry up and down, his eyes squinted in suspicion.

"I hear," Perry said, "that Sam Tryor built this place. Is that right?"

"Yeah," a thirty-year-old woman with crooked gray teeth said. She walked over and stepped in for the kid so he could devote himself full-time to kicking the ground with the toe of his boot. "He built my place. Well, didn't build it. You know, he had it moved here. Put it up on blocks for me. Did my mortgage and all. Got me VA even though my husband ain't been around forever. He's the best."

"Uh-huh," Perry said.

"He helped me when I tried out for the baseball team," a skinny man sitting under a cottonwood tree said. "Believe that? I mean, the guy pitched to me. Threw the ball around. Like in some kind of a McDonald's commercial or something. Shit."

Great, Perry thought, baseball again.

"How long ago these cops come by?" he asked, taking a chance to bond, hoping he wouldn't spoil the Hallmark moment they were deep into.

"They were here almost all night," the woman said. "Telling us they were going to run us in. Run us in, shit. They trashed Sam's house. The dog was barking his head off. Ain't been fed in days, probably. What a mess. And them cops asking where Harry Bronsky was. Saying they was going to run us in. I'll run *them* in. Try me."

"Betty, could you shut the fuck up for five seconds?" said a man who wore black jeans, a black tank top and had a chain that ran from his wallet to his belt.

189

"What do you want, anyway?" he said to Perry. "You going to run us in?"

"Ah, no," Perry said, grinning at the ridiculous phrase *run us in*. "I'm here to check out the house and check on Moreover. The dog—Moreover. I promised Sam's brother Nick I would stop by."

"Yeah, well, they took the dog away," the woman said. "Had to drag him out of there. Let me tell you. That dog, he did *not* want to go. I thought he was going to rip them cops to itty-bitty shreds."

"I'm going to check the place out real quick," Perry said, and walked softly and deferentially to the front door. "You know."

He nodded and smiled a tight smile. He presented his grin to the people near the door like he was showing his hands to an opposing army during a break in battle to exchange medical supplies. The seven self-appointed guardians of my house straightened up and focused on him the same way a mongrel dog snaps its attention on an approaching car.

I'm on their home ground. Their turf, Perry thought, filing *turf* next to *run us in* as another bad figure of speech used today. This place has that fat smell. Like the residue in cars when the windows haven't been opened on a long summer day. Thicker, though.

A breeze pressed out of the low clouds. The odors of beer, urine, humans, exhaust, rotting vinyl and crusty rubber—the smell of Lowly Park—got kicked into the air and diluted. Then, when the wind had moved through, the odors settled back in.

Rain will turn this place into soup, Perry thought. He pictured how the rain would make the park look like a post-apocalypse postcard of ripe summer mud, heat, closeness and steam.

My house had been ripped apart. The couch cushions were upended, the kitchen drawers were on the floor, books were all over the place and dust motes that looked like giant paramecia on a slide floated around.

They didn't find what they were looking for, Perry thought. They probably didn't find anything. You don't find something, anger becomes a reaction. If you're an idiot, or a pack of idiots, you start to rip stuff apart. You don't open drawers, you yank them. You throw them. You look under couch cushions and get mad when there's only change there. Like there should be state secrets or a treasure map with an X because you make the effort to look.

You barely look to see what's what. It goes from trying to find information to leaving a sign you were there—of marking territory, asserting your urgency and need. Cavalry soldiers burned Indian villages after their unsuccessful searches. Romans raped the women. Arizona cops trash double-wides.

You walk into the house of a murderer, it's like going where anyone famous lives—you think some residue will rub off. Maybe you'll feel the ghost of the killer's actions haunting the crannies of the place. The steak knives take on overtones. People. They see movies and television about guys catching a killer. Those guys get shot at, they get witnesses to talk. They befriend the downtrodden, and they beat the pavement, and they rack their brains, and they interview and check files and mug shots and hustle the street people.

But this—this is the real killer-catching. Sure, I got mine, Perry thought. He's dead. Still has to be caught, though. Murdery, murdery death, death, deathly death. Paid to catch. Need his voice on that black box. Need his brain in a jar. Need to find him, and when found, he needs to be cornered. Is he here? Yoo-hoo. Killer guy. Mr. Tryor. You home today?

Yes, I was home.

There was that awful stillness. It was like I was in someone else's house. I had that creepy feeling of disturbing something almost sacred—*another* man's house. *His* castle. Is that an outdated concept?

Perry stamped his foot on the linoleum. He felt thoroughly uncomfortable. He pushed on. He walked in deeper, into the mess left by the frustrated cops. Doors to closets and cabinets were flung open. Papers dribbled out of drawers like guts from an animal. He walked lightly, respectful that he was in someone else's house. He took stock of the mess. Assholes didn't know what they were looking for, he thought. Like I do?

The house has two bedrooms. Perry put it at nine-hundred square feet, tops. It had to be at least twenty-five years old. The color scheme in the kitchen—flat oranges, bad reds, that municipal green, and brown—had been out-of-date since before Perry's first marriage. The Pleather recliner was mustard-colored and shabby.

It was like I had never been there before in my life. I could not relate to the place at all. I hoped I wouldn't get stuck having to haunt it.

There was a film of dust on everything that hadn't been flung. You could see it on the TV best of all. Dust is normal in the desert, but this was another kind of dust, the kind that looked like flakes of human skin. There wasn't anything on the coffee table. Magazines and newspapers had all been thrown and scattered.

There were eight small white bookcases in the living room. There were hundreds of books. Nick said I liked to read. Apparently, I had eclectic and modern tastes as well as an appreciation for the classics. There were all kinds of titles on the spines: novels, new and classic; crime from Hammet to Grisham; plays (Shakespeare to Tennessee Williams), nonfiction and tons of biographies. The books were all sizes and shapes.

There was a framed print of Hopper's *Nighthawks* over the couch.

Sad painting, Perry thought.

There was a photograph of me and Nick on another wall. It must have been his birthday two years ago. They look happy, Perry thought. I have to call Nick Tryor. Check on the dog. Check on Nick. They don't look like brothers, those two. What do we deduce from this, Detective Perry? Perry asked himself in a condescending tone. What facts might we have gained that further enlighten us to the character of our subject, Mr. Tryor?

He read a lot, Perry thought. The books aren't arranged for show. He didn't have guests over often. Only the couch has indentations. He lived here, though, like he was always prepared for guests. He's a straightener, not a cleaner. He was probably a nervous man. He wasn't into status. That television is old. What else?

Perry walked farther into house, to the kitchen. There was a dog leash wrapped around a chair leg. There was a chewed piece of wood nearby. Part of the paneled cabinet had been clawed at.

Moreover had the run of the place, Perry thought. This was a comfortable house. This was a comfortable man. Comfortable with his dog and himself.

What were they hoping to find in my house?

In Jeffrey Dahmer's house they found metal drums filled with acid. They found femurs floating inside. Manual Noriega had the usual tacky collection of Nazi symbols, Hitler paraphernalia and pornography. They must give out that stuff to deposed strongmen at a camp they go to. I suppose in a murderer's house the police expect to find evidence of murderous intent left on the nightstand, like reading material.

That must be why people paused near this place,
and paused as they passed the Pizza Man. They must
imagine there will be some substance that will brush
off on them if they get close enough. Maybe if they go
close enough to the belongings of a killer, it would tell
them why.

The homes of killers, though, probably look like anyone else's house. They're homes with old high school
yearbooks, utility bills under refrigerator magnets,
bookmarks, magazines, toothpaste, remote controls, a
telephone, books, clothing. These normal things take
on insinuations when you know who they belonged to.
Perhaps that's all a haunted house is—the feelings that
the living assign to the dead because they think they
should.

Silverware, coupons, letters, newspaper inserts,
Coke cans left for recycling, empty dog food bags, and
a mess of other material—the collection of stuff anyone gains during life—was spread throughout the
kitchen.

Sam was a soup man, Perry thought, looking at the
cans of vegetable and tomato Campbell's soup in the
open cabinets. I went through my soup phases, Lord
knows.

In the bedroom, the bed was made. Perry looked
under it because he knew he would be tense all day if
he didn't. It's one of those places you have to look.
Even little kids know that.

The drawers of a filing cabinet were open. The lock
had been picked—there were scratches that looked like
they were from a knife all around it. Those guys probably had a contest to see who was man enough to open
the thing, Perry thought.

Inside the drawers of the filing cabinet were porno
magazines and movies. I cringed. Perry didn't examine
them. He'd seen enough of those in his day, too.

There's always the same old stash places for that material. The discrete nooks. The nookie nooks. Between the box spring and the mattress, the top shelf of the linen closet, a box in the back of a closet or under the bed in the dead center, in a shed outside. The magazines and the videos in the locked filing cabinet meant Sam was bashful about those habits.

"This guy's so normal, I want to throw up," Perry said.

I felt like I was getting away with something.

Perry stood in my bedroom and wanted to lie down. He didn't, though. He knew better. If he did, if he put himself on my bedspread and stared up at the same ceiling that I used as a blank canvas to think my thoughts, then he would be soiled by the experience.

I'm still a cop, he thought. This guy's a murdering motherfucker. The life of this poor, dumb bastard can be reduced to this one act because it is the most profound act he has committed. And he holds the new record, don't forget. He killed those people. All those people. Murdery murder, deathly death. No good, goddamned reason for it. I need to find that dog. I got things to do. This place makes me sick.

◦⊸⊙

I wasn't at my house. My soul was with Nick and with Perry and at the Pizza Man. My whole life was the brief time I spent with a gun. That was all that mattered.

Perry rushed out of the house. The moment he got outside the seven guardians closed in around him. They stared at him with their mouths open. They looked like cats when they get a scent. They waited for him to speak.

"Fucked up," Perry said.

The seven people nodded just like people do on a subway platform or in a doorway during a rainstorm. They nodded for no reason, with no reasoning, only to make a fake connection for a moment before they moved on.

"They took DNA samples. You could see the fog stuff coming off the tubes when they came out," a kid with a bag of Cool Ranch Doritos said. "Like in the movies."

"Just like," a girl said. She was maybe fourteen, looked seventeen, and acted thirty-two.

"They? Cops, you mean?" Perry said.

"Them. They. Cops."

"When, exactly?"

"Yesterday. Last night," the Cool Ranch kid said. "They were all over this place. Should have seen it. Something else. Hundreds of cops. I had to flush so much shit. It was fucked up. That many cops. Gave me the willies. They took Harry Bronsky. They said it was his guns used in the shooting."

"How's that?" Perry said.

"Mr. Tryor was holding them for Harry," the kid said.

"Harry couldn't keep them?"

"Hell, no."

"Why not?"

"He's on probation is why not," Cool Ranch said. "They took Harry right on outta here. So many cops. Really gave me the willies. You're really big, mister. Play any ball?"

"Me, too. Gave me the willies," the girl said.

"Yeah," Perry said. "Me, too."

While he was driving to the station, Perry saw a bumper sticker on a Mercedes: IF YOU'RE NOT OUTRAGED, YOU'RE NOT PAYING ATTENTION. That sticker made more sense to Walter Perry than anything he had read before in his life.

Then he saw another sticker on a Nova that said SAVE THE WORLD. KILL YOURSELF. He agreed with that one, too.

❧

"Hello, Walt," Chief Samson said. "Sit down." The chief was on the phone, and it looked like he was on it against his will. He covered the mouthpiece and said, "I'm on with the Feds."

He was hunched over and looked like he usually looked when he had to take orders. Perry thought Chief Samson was a fair enough man, one who didn't like to take orders but who always obeyed them. That's because the chief was not a bright man. He was neither learned nor creative. He was merely fair. To Perry, that attribute made Samson very nearly a great man.

The chief looked beat. He looked beyond tired. His skin was gray.

"Uh-huh," Chief Samson said into the phone, looking at a spot far away on a wall. "Yes, I agree. One thousand million percent...I think we all feel the same way...I can tell you...I can...I...Yes. Well, I can tell you...Sure. Hey. If you would shut up then I could tell you...Yes. It's been a long night. That was completely out of line...I agree...Thank you...Immediately."

Chief Samson held the phone in the air over the hook for a very long time. He held it there so long it became less a phone and more like a formless shape. He filled Perry in. The task force had disintegrated. The station was still staked out by the press, though no longer surrounded. The Department of Public Safety and Homeland Security had taken over the case.

"Having a joyous morning?" Perry said, gently relieving Chief Samson of the phone.

"State and fed guys. Incredible. They have plaster tracks of footprints. And tire tread prints. And dog prints."

197

"Dog prints. Cute."

"They interviewed the dog."

"Moreover?"

"Huh?"

"The dog's name is Moreover. They interviewed the dog?"

"Animal psychologist. Two vets. They got this guy, one of those trainers with the padded sleeve, to see if the dog tries to rip it apart so they can tell if it's been trained to kill and maim."

"Was it?"

"No. That dog—Moroner? Nicest animal anyone's seen since Lassie saved Timmy from the well. They put five guys in there with it for three hours to find out it's the sweetest doggy in the world. I told Barbara Cloven—from the paper?—all about it. Wait till the state guys and the feds see it in the paper. Or not. She's such a dumb bitch, anyway."

The two men laughed then became silent.

"Where's the dog now?" Perry asked. "Can I get it, for the guy's brother?"

"Sure. It's at the pound."

More silence.

"This is a record," Chief Samson said. "No one died overnight. Docs say it'll stay at forty, not counting our shooter. Goddamn, I am tired. A record. Here. The previous high was something like thirty-five, in Australia. That's the other side of the world. I am so beat."

"What's the next move?"

"Give the state all your notes, or whatever. Let's get out of this business. It's a bad business anyway. My neck has this creak—crick?—in it so tight. Jesus."

"I was out at Tryor's house today."

"Yeah, I know. There's going to be a news conference. Montan says we should do it tomorrow. He says it'll rain. Says that looks good. Dramatic. Standing in the rain. That's what we'll do."

"Somber," Perry said. "Very 'Streets of Laredo.'"

"Exactly our thinking. They're going to have the place cleaned tonight—the restaurant. I'm getting crap about how we should have left the bodies in their seats or where they lay. The investigation. Believe that? Could you have imagined? People in there all night. Cold. Blood hardening. Anyway. Place gets cleaned. There's already been a guy with a camera in there. I move my ankle, it cracks. Every time. Weird. So."

"So."

The two men looked at one another.

"Is it hard, being black?" Samson asked Perry.

"Hard? No. It's easy. I wake up every morning and do it all day, no sweat. It's when I have to be white that it gets a little tricky."

There was no laughter. The world felt stuck in its spin.

"Well," Perry said. "Who do I talk to?"

"Me. Tell me. What do you know?"

Perry leaned back in his hard little chair. He realized there was no there there. There was no smoking gun, no clear explanation. He'd known it since yesterday, but for the first time, he said it to himself in so many words: There's no reason. He was comforted by that truth.

He's a guy went and had a bad day. For the home team. Perry smiled and worried he was losing his mind.

"Regular guy," Perry said. "A normal guy. Really. Fifty-two-year-old white man. Owned his own business—Your Owned Home—selling double-wides. People who knew him liked him. Member of the Chamber of Commerce. No violent history. No record. Served in the army four years. That's how he came out here, like, thirty years ago. My sources say Tryor did nothing particularly sensitive, or strange, on post. No special projects. I spoke with his brother Nick. Nick's a millionaire. From selling rocks, of all things. Says his brother was normal. I don't know a better word. No signs of anything weird at Tryor's house."

"Fringe? Freemen? Waco? Oklahoma? Revenge against OJ? Osama?"

"Nope. No literature. None of the signs. Weren't even his guns."

"Yeah. They worked that kid from Lowly Park over pretty good. Says he gave Sam Tryor the guns to hold. Stuck to that. The guns were legal, anyway."

"My theory on that is the locks on Tryor's truck don't work. It's an old piece of junk. He was holding the guns for the kid and probably didn't want them to get stolen from his truck."

"A humanitarian, how nice. What about personal problems?"

"Nothing. No recent divorce. No woman troubles I know about. No men troubles, either."

"Woman named Dottie Supre, Tryor's girlfriend?" the chief said. "She went on the *Today* show with Matt Lauer this morning."

"Didn't catch it."

"She says Tryor was an odd case. She says he tried out for plays here and wasn't cast. Says he didn't like people. The afternoon paper is going with some of that, too. TV's already got it. About how this guy is the Failed Actor Murderer. They say he didn't get a part in a play and got mad. You ever get that stiffness in your fingers before it rains? I hate that."

"Nice theory. The actor bit. I don't see it, but, hey, what do I know."

"Five people in that restaurant were armed. Two got their guns out. You'd have thought out of that many one—*one*—would have got him. Didn't even get a shot off."

"You'd have thought at least one. But it happened in about three minutes. Three minutes with someone pointing a gun around is a lot of time to do nothing much more than be scared."

"What about medical? Terminal cancer, diabetes, AIDS, bad cold, anything?"

"I didn't see a lot of meds in the bathroom. I'll get on that."

"Nah, don't bother."

"Okay."

There was a fat silence.

"Walt, what happened in there?"

"I don't know, Chief."

"Walt, what the hell happened in there with this guy?"

Perry zoned out. He started to form a theory about me and about the shooting. Then he lost what it was about. He thought about the song at the morgue. Sinatra. It was Frank. Once he knew the name of that song, then, and only then, would he let himself forget the whole sad mess from these sad, messy days.

"Walt?" Chief Samson said, snapping his fingers. "Walter. You with me here?"

"Chief, I saw a bumper sticker today that said, 'If You're Not Outraged, You're Not Paying Attention.' That's what I think happened in there."

"Someone wasn't paying attention?"

"Tryor was outraged. Mad. He'd had enough, and he started shooting, and he killed a bunch of people."

Chief Samson leaned back in his chair and looked at Perry. His eyes melted into a new expression, his shoulders relaxed. His mouth opened, but he didn't say anything for a few seconds.

"That's fine," he said. "Tell you what, Walt. I'll talk to the state and the feds."

"You want a report?"

"I think I got it. Outrage. I'll let them know. Go home. Get some sleep. And, Walt, take some time. You have vacation."

"I have to pick up the dog first."

"Sure. Take Moron home. Take the time. We'll talk later."

"We'll say Tryor's a nut, right?" Perry said with his back to the chief as he walked toward the door. "We'll say he had a fight with his girlfriend. He didn't get cast in a play. He was suffering post-traumatic stress syndrome. He's a wacko, and now he's dead, and all those poor people. All those poor people."

The door closed. Chief Samson heard Perry talking outside in the hall, and he wondered if, when the rain came, the popping in his knees every time he got up would finally stop.

—13—

A heavy rain passed through Bisbee. The ground was soaked, and a river of water ran down Brewery Gulch into an open mine shaft.

Nick and I used to go to Bisbee years ago when it was nothing but a clapped-out mining town. The mines had closed, and you could live rent-free. It had great bars and an art opening every weekend for anyone—with or without talent. The town was recently discovered by tourists from California and had pretty much become a rustic tourist trap. But Nick still thought of it as a getaway.

There was a house key waiting for him at the Copper Queen bar. At the house was a bottle of Chivas and one glass set out as a bathroom doorstop. By four a.m., the Chivas was mostly gone, and Nick sat on the floor, almost asleep as he drank and cried and listened to the wind blow in, then out, of town.

He was trying to decide whether he should hate me and tell the world he hated me. He had every reason to do both.

He woke up at nine a.m. with all his nerve endings swollen from a bad sleep. Screams night cut lights all dead, he thought. He lit a cigarette and felt like he could vomit from his eyeballs. Mornings like that, days when I came to rather than woke up, was why I quit drinking.

Nick straightened up. He made some eggs. His head hurt, but he kept his food down. He took a shower. He tried to act normal when he shaved, but he didn't look himself in the eye as he scraped the lather. Everything looked terrible and idle in the gray June light.

A winter light, Nick thought. A tea-sipping day. Door slam walk open sit clutch shoot scream step. Three minutes on TV. Just say Sam was a twisted psycho, and I'm free.

He closed the front door and started on a walk. Nothing felt real to him. He descended fifty-seven steps down to the street and headed up Tombstone Canyon. Everything was subdued in the rainy mist. He felt small and invisible among the tourists who looked into the shops and held their umbrellas. Stab cut dig gash huts mother screams sirens questions.

Nick had a hole in one sneaker, and it made the inside slimy and cold with water against his foot. There are worse things, he thought. Much worse.

A few steps later, he considered where he might go. Nowhere, he decided. He was liberated by the idea. *Nowhere at all. No plans. This could be the start of a new me. Happy-go-lucky Nick Tryor. He's been so devil-may-care since his brother shot all those people.* Breaking cuts fall crunch thud squirt gush. *What if I left today? Disappeared. Like the children in Bogota. I have the money. I can take $200,000 in cash. I can! Who's to stop me?*

Up ahead of Nick was Saint Patrick's Church. It had beige bricks, and was faintly municipal-looking. It sat on Quality Hill, where in the old days the quality people lived. It was the high ground. Hot nails smoke broken wounds, Nick thought.

Before we grew up, Nick was Catholic. We had a childhood of abject poverty, totems, stories and ghoulish rituals of eating body parts and drinking blood. We would get sent off to church each Sunday. We were given four bits for the poor box. I instigated a revolt, and one day, instead of giving our money to the local winos through the church, I took Nick to sip sodas and eat pretzel sticks at Irish Mary's soda fountain. My life as a career criminal got off to a rocky start when we screwed up on how long mass lasted and came home early. We got a beating when Nick spilled the beans, but we never had to go to church again.

Nick walked up five steps and stood in front of Saint Patrick's open door. He looked inside. He thought about going in and confessing to what he was going to do, confessing to his planned lie about me to the world.

It was cool and dark. The altar was dirty-blond wood. There was a man inside moving around reverently. He had just lit a candle. He was wearing what passes for businessman's casual clothing—short-sleeved button-down shirt and brown creased...what do they call them?...slacks! Nick stood in the mist and peered in, but he decided not to go inside. He thought it would be better to keep on walking. He considered making up a whole new him and leaving for someplace where no one knew who he or I was. Whole and new. Him!

Throat blood hot wash red open dying, he thought.

He didn't think about me. He wanted to put me behind him.

Nick stopped on a little bridge that spanned a wash running alongside Main Street. *Leave. Go. Now.* Teal-colored water slithered down the wash. A rock cut a ridge in the rushing water, an angle in the flow. *Go east. New York.*

He started walking back toward town. *Rent an apartment. Take maybe a suitcase, a toothbrush, one suit.*

Be alone. Nick felt fragile, scared and angry about the choices open to him. He imagined his disappearance, and gained comfort from the idea. His age disappeared from his mind. The last few days were wiped away.

I have no age, he thought. No identity. I will live a meager life and starve if I have to. I'll leave a note so the business is taken care of. I should have an attorney go over everything. No. New me. If there's a problem...who cares?

He passed a woman on the sidewalk. She carried an umbrella designed to look like the front page of the Fort Worth *Star Telegram*. She stopped. She searched for something in her purse. She jammed her hand into it and tried to balance the newspaper umbrella as she did so. Meaningless. How meaningless, Nick thought.

I wondered what he would do. It was important.

I can be an exile, Nick thought. I am already outside society, thanks to Sam.

He watched the woman with the umbrella scowl up at the rain then down at her purse because whatever she was looking for was not at hand.

Why do I live with these people and care about their needs, about the thing they can't find, the intrusion of weather and the patterns of sun in a room? Nick thought. In fact, I only want dark. I want the rain in puddles and a tiny stream alongside the street.

A raindrop landed on his eye. *Leave now and everyone—the police!—would have to wonder where I was.* He imagined he was the star of a drama. The stress got to him, they would say. Perhaps he flipped. Simply lost it. Nick liked the idea.

He looked up and found himself near the steps to the house where he was staying. This is an important flight of steps to someone, he thought. He didn't want to go up yet. He had nothing to do, and he didn't want to do nothing because that made him think.

He leaned back against a metal handrail. The rain on it soaked through his clothes and chilled him. He lit a cigarette. Slit red dark spurting.

I feel like James Dean, Nick thought.

People-watching was not a sport he did well because he never did it. He was too self-conscious. Plus, he thought it was boring.

I used to people watch all the time. When we were kids, I was always pointing somebody out to Nick. I gave them motives and put dialogue in their mouths. Nick thought I was a little nuts, and he would get bothered when I was mean to the people I watched. I would call some of them fat, stupid, dumb. I didn't do it often, usually when I was in a bad mood or tired. My cynical side would emerge. Like in anybody. And it was funny. Sometimes.

Nick didn't touch the railing with his hands. That would get the cigarettes wet. He stood and tried to look like he was waiting for someone.

A woman crossed the street with a group of people. She walked slowly. Her back was to Nick. Nice ass, he thought, startling himself with the coarseness. Then he said it out loud: "Nice ass." He thought about moving to a beach community.

The woman looked into a shop window up the street. Her hair hid her face from him.

Sam must have been in a bad mood that day, Nick thought. Forty people. I will never be comfortable with this. Any of this. No aspect of this. Forty. Do I recover the body or do the police deliver it? Is there a special man for that? Did I give them my address? Who do I invite? Why was he so angry?

If he could just see the woman's nose, he'd be able to tell what she looked like.

She and her group went into a store. A family crossed the street directly toward him. At first glance, they seemed like a Vitamin D-added, good-looking family. They could have come straight out of a book of statistics compiled by a commercial casting agent. Like people from an advertisement.

The dad was tall. He had on tan shorts and Nikes. The wife had a bit of a tummy, and she wore makeup that, on a bright day, might have looked good. In the drizzle, her made-up face was a separate, free-floating aberration of hideousness—glops of red and green looked like they were swimming on her skin. This woman, Nick thought. She is a disgusting pig. He surprised himself. Leave, and I'll have my independence, a room somewhere, a gut-level lifestyle. Go on TV and call him a nut. Either way, I win.

The children in the family were coming toward him. The boy carefully skipped the puddles. He must've been about nine. His sister was in her early teens. She feared the puddles and concentrated to avoid any part of them getting near her gleaming pink running shoes.

Everything about them was careful, studied, purposeful.

Nick flicked his cigarette between his thumb and index finger, and it landed in a puddle and hissed out. The woman and her friends came out of the shop. They milled around one another like huge electrons. The woman hadn't turned toward Nick. She hadn't given him an opportunity to see her. He kept looking at her and waited for her to turn.

Be beautiful, Nick thought. Please. Today be someone I need. I could love you. I could take you with me, and we could talk and suck on silences, and you could rely on me and I wouldn't have to rely on you, not really. Maybe the beach somewhere—anywhere but Texas, Nick thought, inventing the conversation in which he charmed her and took her away. Not Texas.

Not Florida. South, though. Mexico. *I wish I had learned Spanish. All this time in Arizona, and I don't know Spanish, but I like Mexican food. Maybe* she *knows Spanish.*

He lined up possible jokes and opening lines to use on this woman on the sidewalk. *Perhaps she's visiting, visiting a tourist town she doesn't know because she doesn't like her life, and who does these days, anyway, who really likes where they are every day with people talking about the weather and about how terrible when they would be better off silent?*

Alarms went off in Nick's head. They sounded like loud clanging. Things sped up a notch as his plans become more desperate, more detailed.

The woman walked away from him on her tanned legs. Everything about her was translucent bronze. He felt better that he hadn't seen her face. He could build her as he wanted her to be. Maybe he would go out later and see her in a bar. There would be a one-sided history already. He would sit in a corner and nurse a beer. Even better, he would swirl a serious drink. Brandy would be perfect. Brandy in a small snifter, and a pack of Dunhills. He would sit there and let his eyes saunter...

The woman turned her profile, and Nick saw her.

How did they see the hit down fall thump bleed then?

Nick stood with his hand on the wet railing and looked at her lips and nose. He looked at all this woman was not. An older woman instead came toward him, and their eyes met for that instant of not meaning it but you smile anyway, like when you brush a thigh and excuse yourself slightly.

"It's like they never heard of Sir Walter Raleigh," the woman said to Nick.

He screwed his smile tighter.

"Nope," he answered, not having a clue what she was talking about. "No, it's like they haven't."

The woman was wrinkled and pinched. She passed by him, tightly clutching her umbrella to protect herself from the rain as though it were a virus sent by some government. She nodded to him. He seemed familiar to her, but she didn't know why. *Our picture in the paper and* Newsweek *and on the television news.*

It was everywhere.

Nick was cold. His lungs ached from smoking too much, but he convinced himself that Bisbee's mile-high altitude was the thing hurting him, and lit another. The misty rain had turned brittle; the drops that hit his eyelashes were now a bother. *I am a round little man standing in the rain. In the round little rain. Yeah, a beach house.*

He started for the house, then spun around to go back to the store for another pack of cigarettes. Long as I'm out, he thought. Clack crunch. Bodies hitting the floor. Did the building shake? Do you think you'll die? Does your life flash? Did Sam plan it? Spur-of-the-moment thing? Blood in the throat. The taste. Hot and thick.

After the store, Nick hurried home. He thought about the things he had to do. *Funeral.*

He didn't know exactly what to do about my funeral, but he knew he had to do something. I knew he would do the right thing, whatever he did. That held true for whether he went into hiding or went on TV. Whatever he did was fine and good.

The woman from before walked alongside Nick. Her friends trailed in tow. She said something to them about going this way because she wanted to see what there was to buy on that side of town. Nick tried to speed up and put some distance between himself and who he'd thought he could become a few minutes ago.

She kept pace, then rushed ahead of him and her friends to scout out their path.

She stopped and looked back at her friends. Nick hated her in that second when she stood there with her hand on her hip and her head tilted in that impatient way as she implored her friends to hurry. She glanced at him, made eye contact, then immediately looked away.

She knows, Nick thought. She knows.

He hated her for who he had made her into when she was, after all, only average. He walked past her to the steps that led up to the place where he was staying. Bang bang dead. Bang. The loss. The loss?

❧

Once he was in the house, he threw the cigarettes on the coffee table. He flopped down on the couch and turned the television on. He wanted a beer, but he was out of beer. There was no way he was going out there to get more. He wasn't even going to reach up and turn the lights on. He turned the TV off.

My funeral.

If you need anything...

I'm so sorry, really. If there's ever anything...

Feel free to call on us. Anytime. Day, night...

He was a good man.

What can I say?

Our prayers are with you.

The squeeze of a hand around the upper arm. Eyes not meeting eyes. Food cooked. The offer of support, extended by rote and with unspoken assurance it wouldn't be accepted. The bowed heads. The tense face muscles. The respectful, library-like whispering. The strange limelight the loved ones of departed loved ones bask in from the attention and sympathy bestowed.

There won't be any of that, Nick thought. There won't be a real funeral for Sam. He sat and tried think-

211

ing of a decision he could come to about what to do—about me, about what I did and who I was. He decided not to go on TV and not to leave. He would ride it out and be who he was. The same old Nick.

He thought about the things you do at funerals, the things you say, the precious banalities he wouldn't hear. Because of what Sam did, he will have to be buried in secret, Nick thought. Because he stood in the Pizza Man restaurant and unloaded. Because—say it—he shot and killed forty people. Innocent people. Because I can't get my mind around it. I think it and think it harder until it seems mushy and I can get a grip, but I'm not even at the corner of its bigness. I'm feeling sorry for myself. How big this is.

I can bury him once they release the body. Yes. How do I do that, bury someone in secret? Don't the authorities have to know where and when? Should I send out invitations to the funeral? Do I call a priest or the chief of police to officiate?

As the day and the house got dark, I looked at my brother for the last time. I loved him so much. I wanted him to turn on a light and not sit in the dark. I wanted so much for him. I wanted him to be happy.

Nick did not forgive me, because he didn't blame me for anything. He loved me. He always had. He always would. Nothing had changed.

He turned a light on and felt better.

—14—

*J*erome Fisher haunted millions of people. He died of a stroke at the age of thirty-seven while he sat at his keyboard and worked on a video game called *Me-gaDeath Rampage: The Final Page*. His previous game was *MegaDeath Rampage*.

Fisher knew that some people wanted to be able to kill other people, and he made a mint off it. (I was one of the few people to *actually* do something about it, but that's a different story.). The player in each game went through a neighborhood and shot people. Cops, mothers, families, anyone. The catch? Anyone the player targeted might also have a gun. The player got points whenever they killed an innocuous-looking person who was really packing heat without getting shot themselves,. They lost points if they killed someone who was a regular person. If you shot a man dressed as a priest but he was carrying a Mac-10, you got points. If you shot a guy dressed as a priest who was on his way to church unarmed, you lost points.

After he slumped over his laptop and died, Fisher became a ghost in his own machine. He appeared in the game as a character that could not be killed and who went in and just killed everyone. The player was unable to play. Players tried to kill Fisher, but they couldn't because he was a ghost. The company that made the game had no explanation for the ghost and they couldn't fix it. Five months after his death, *MegaDeath Rampage: The Final Page* was pulled from the shelves, and the company went bankrupt.

Fisher, meanwhile, is still in the game killing innocent and dangerous alike, not caring which is which, to save them from the lunatics who bought the game.

The rain came to Sierra Vista. Then it continued to come. Small planes were ordered grounded. The rain descended, and everyone seemed to forget how to drive their cars. Arizonans drove in the rain the way everyone else drove in the snow, and they drove Perry up a wall.

National weather people chuckled over how Arizona was being battered with the unseasonable rain, and said, "Yes, but it's a dry rain."

Ramon, at the morgue, thought about how the rain would soften the ground for all the digging of all the graves for all the bodies of all the people who had been shot.

I knew I should have replaced my windshield wipers, Perry thought, barely able to see as he drove slowly around town. For some reason, he was unable to leave the town limits. He'd put himself on vacation, and it was open-ended leave for up to five weeks, but he made no plans to leave.

I hate my own house, he thought as he drove. Why don't I leave? I wish I knew that song playing in the morgue. I feel if I could get that song, I will have learned something. I wish I had replaced my wipers. I can barely see. I should get that dog up at the pound for Nick Tryor. That poor guy. I should go and at least see it.

He thought about the news conference. *Closure, that's the word. They told me to go back to that liquor store after I got shot, after that kid pocked up my face. Sonofabitch. Man, I'm in a bad mood. The barometric pressure is killing me behind the eyes.*

They didn't call it closure back then. They didn't have that word circulating among the general population. They said it would be a good thing to go there so I could put it behind me. Closure. No one used the word utilize, *either, did they? I hate that word. Worse than nigger. Utilize. That's where it starts. Right there. Utilize. We can utilize the information. People wondering all the time, "How'd the world get so complicated? Where did it all start?" Right there. Utilize. That's how.*

Perry stared at the police scanner under his dash. He watched it for a long time and heard nothing as he drove down Fry Boulevard toward the Pizza Man.

I am steering the car. I am looking through the windshield, he thought, remembering my alleged AA calming device. It really works! Amazing. I'm more settled already. At least I got something from this case.

I have to say, though, I never went to AA, and I never used that as a calming device. Nick must have made that up.

I remembered more and more things now. My life was coming back to to me.

Perry came up on the Pizza Man. He knew he was there without even looking to see where he was. Its presence reached out and clutched at him. He parked and lit a cigarette.

I love the rain. The new season approaching. Feeling the year pull on its new clothing.

His Thermos of coffee put a comforting stain of steam on his windshield. He wrote Winsome's name with his fingernail there, then he watched it get covered with new hotness. He wrote *Moreover*. The rain splat-tered on the ledge of the open car window and splashed him every so often.

I am officially on vacation for five weeks, as of this moment. Relax. I am looking at the umbrellas and lights across the street. Where is everyone? I see the flowers piled at the entrance.

He thought the colors from the flowers were garish. They looked staged, he thought. He hummed the morgue tune. If only I had the words. Now I sound like a Glenn Campbell song.

Lieutenant Montan looked embarrassed by the low turnout at the news conference, Cops outnumbered reporters. The reporters had moved on to cover the kidnapping of a cardboard company heiress in California. She had been taken by environmentalists, and they had demands.

What if they gave a news conference and nobody came? Perry wondered with a laugh and a sip of coffee. If a reporter fell over in the forest and no microphones were there to hear it, would he make a noise?

"Now that everyone who is going to be here is here, we can begin," Montan said. "We are here to announce the results of an exhaustive investigation conducted by four state and federal agencies, and the Sierra Vista Police Department. We spent over three hundred man-hours investigating the Memorial Day Massacre here at this location. We have come to the following conclusions."

Tryor had his reasons, Perry thought. No, wait. He chased the thought around in his mind. It was a thought that might lead to the answer about what happened and why. If it wasn't the answer, at least it might be an answer.

Then I could trot on over across the street and tell those reporters what happened. Like the grizzled, all-knowing, rebellious, brilliant, burnt-out maverick detective at the end of

*any Hollywood movie who sticks it to his gruff superiors.
Bullshit. Now I forgot what I was thinking about. Damn.*

"Sam Tryor acted alone," Montan said. "Even
though they were not his guns utilized in the killings, he
worked in cooperation with no one in the planning or
in the execution of the crime. He received no assis-
tance in carrying out this incident.

"The final count is forty dead, and the shooter.
Twenty-one people were wounded." He paused appro-
priately. "The latest available technology, including the
FBI's crime lab in Washington DC, was employed to
analyze the contents of Mr. Tryor's residence. Our
findings are that Mr. Tryor appears to have had a fascination with killing. Many books devoted to the subject
of mass murder, including on David Berkowitz, Zodiac
and Hitler, were found in Mr. Tryor's residence. Fur-
thermore…"

They're making it up, Perry realized. They're inventing it. No wonder no one trusts cops. No code.
There is no code. No rules. No higher being to answer
to. That's why. That must be why he did it.

"Associates of Mr. Tryor's have revealed, and our
psychologists have confirmed, that, in addition to his
fascination with murder and death, Mr. Tryor suffered
from an intense and negative superiority complex. Mr.
Tryor believed he was better than the people he killed.
Obviously.

"Mr. Tryor spoke of his hatred for people in general to one young lady in particular, and to acquain-
tances. In diaries recovered from Mr. Tryor's residence,
he states he no longer trusts the government, he thinks
humanity will be responsible for its own doom, and he
says, in so many words, that he can't take it any longer.
Those are direct quotes. That is all. Are there any questions?"

Perry was right, they'd made it up.

They don't know, Perry thought. They have no code. They don't care. It's another public shooting. Every day. They happen every day now. It's so common we call it "going postal." Usually it's four or five people. It's in an office building or a park or a lobby. In schools. So many schools. Amish schools. We joke about the disgruntled gunman. About the scope and the tower and the gun. It's another public shooting. Sam Tryor, I think, had enough. He knows there is no God here. There isn't any Thou Shalt Not. That's the way it goes.

I whispered two words into Perry's ear to finish his thought: *That's Life*.

Perry slapped the side of his car with his large open hand. It went *pop!*

Ellen Barkin!

That's life. That's what people say. Riding high in April...shot down in May! He took a sip of coffee. He was so happy to have finally remembered the name of the song, he considered his day complete.

⤜⤏

Frank Sinatra. Those were the days. Cities were good places to live. Tryor in Detroit. Maybe he liked Frank, Perry thought. Who doesn't? Sam Tryor grew up when you didn't speak back to your parents. I don't know. That's got something to do with it, though. I don't know why the guy did it. Maybe *he* doesn't know.

I don't blame the poor bastard. I really don't. That's what's been missing here. I admire the guy. That's not good. I hate him, too, sure. Forty people dead. Were they important people? No, probably not. They are now, though. The governor and the president are saying we shall always remember them. Used the word *shall*.

Were they nice people? No nicer, no meaner than anyone else. I'd give every one of them the finger if they cut me off on the highway. These people were nothing special. Sam Tryor's nothing special. I hate him. But, in a way, you've got to hand it to him. You have to. That's life. That's what people say.

⌘

Perry watched the cops and the reporters. Silently, they packed. Wordlessly, they left. The rain beat down on the windows of the restaurant. There was a big sign that announced the Pizza Man would open up again next Monday.

The rain beat down on a tarp thrown over the flowers and the stuffed animals and the cards and the clippings and the photographs in front of the restaurant. The cover for the makeshift shrine sagged under the downpour. Perry watched it and got sadder and sadder.

He thought about what he'd just seen happen at the news conference. He thought about how he would probably see a lot of things in the future that would explain why I did what I did. There were no excuses for it, but there were reasons. And they would each make perfect sense.

Perry stayed across the street from the restaurant for another hour. He smoked and drank coffee from his Thermos. Then he left for animal control to collect Moreover and take him home.

I would never see Perry again.

―15―

I was at the Pizza Man for the last time. I would be going soon. I was glad to have a look, glad for the chance to put a few last pieces together.

The place was more than a mess. It was covered with the leftovers of mayhem. It was, for some odd reason, more pathetic than finding all those condoms on a beach.

The Pizza Man was dark. It was eleven-thirty Tuesday night. There was a man with a bucket in the restaurant.

Carl Maxwell figured the job would take six hours. He was the owner and sole employee of Maxwell's BioHazard and Disposals. He knew it wouldn't be an easy job. He dimly made out the particulars in the enormous room of the restaurant. It would be illuminated just from the streetlights. The electricity had been cut. Who knew why. Maxwell didn't.

A group of local business people, not even the owners of the restaurant, had hired him to clean the place. Maxwell had heard the story before—the smell, people had started to come and collect gruesome souvenirs, the business people said they needed to move on and put it behind them for the good of the com-

221

munity. Doris Lambert, from the Sierra Vista Convention and Visitor's Bureau, paid him up front. She didn't even look him in the eye. They rarely did, but Maxwell thought she was worse than most.

"How much is this? Here's a check," she said. "Thank you. Here are the keys. When you're done, let yourself out."

Even in the low light, Maxwell and I saw blood in what, to him, were familiar patterns. There were drag marks made by bleeding people who'd pulled themselves along, and by the dead as they were removed. There were smears, pools and splatter. He shined his flashlight on rings. He swung it around and lit up cards from wallets, half-eaten food, a cold cut hero with bite marks, one shoe. He thought about photographs he'd seen of the thousands of shoes from Holocaust victims. It was worse than seeing the bodies.

Gunshots, screams, cries all echoed from the walls, the floor, the tables, the white corky drop ceiling and the pipes above it.

It was here, Maxwell thought. This is a kind of holy ground now. There is the reverb of awful history here. Picture yourself standing still on the grassy knoll, in front of the ovens, at the bare plot of land where the Murrah Building stood, outside the high school in Littleton, Colorado, and in the craters off Center Street in lower Manhattan. At those places, and so many more, you can feel the shockwaves of the terrible days impact your unmoving body and your mind.

Maxwell had traveled to Dallas to see where Kennedy was shot. He'd been to Ground Zero. Each location was quiet as a church. They were almost religious experiences. He planned to drive to Oklahoma City later in the summer. If business continued to go well, he hoped to visit to Poland and Germany in the fall.

They're actually paying me to see this scene, Maxwell thought as he looked around at the detritus from the latest tragedy he had been hired to make right. Ah, well.

Maxwell was a stocky yet surprisingly young and handsome man. He put his bucket down. He hated to get philosophical on the job. It distracted him. My job is about stains, he thought. About deep spillage and biological matter.

He pulled a rubber apron over his head. The full-body smock made him look as blunt and thoughtless as the men who work in slaughterhouses, or like the villain in a teen horror movie. He put a protective mask over his face and felt like he was an extra in an instructional video about civil disaster preparedness. He smacked thick rubber gloves snug onto his hands. In all this blood are the pathogens. AIDS. Hepatitis. Ebola. Hantavirus. Legionnaires. Who knows what all. Got to wear protection so this stuff doesn't get you. It's not good if murdered people kill you after they're dead. Nothing noble in that.

All right. This is exactly like a suicide cleanup, he thought. There's bigger stains, more matter. That's all.

Maxwell steeled himself to his task and inhaled deeply, the way a kid will suck in his breath before he jumps in a cold lake, or kisses his fat aunt on Thanksgiving.

Get it over with, he thought. He could taste the acrid, heavy, bloody chemical smell on the back ridge of his sinuses. When I am done, no one will know anything happened here. Not a soul.

～≈◊

I don't think this site will endure, Maxwell thought sadly as he wrung a bloody Handi-Wipe out into his yellow bucket and looked around the large, gray, cold restaurant. This won't become a spot of pilgrimage. It's too common.

These shootings, public shootings. Guys going crazy in a restaurant or an office building or at the post office. So many times, now, at schools. Every day, it seems. It's a shame. It's not history. It's not tragedy. The lesson, if there ever was one, is so diluted. It is not the poetry of human struggle against evil. It's just a bummer.

He straightened up and stretched his back. Now that the major blood spills were mopped up, he took the broom and started to put the furniture back in place. He swept as he went along. He got under tables and behind dividers. Sometimes, he would find chips of bone, little parts of fingers, chunks of skin. *Got to get those. Someone finds that later, when they're eating, there's a lawsuit for sure.*

Maxwell always felt weird in places where people had killed themselves or others. Where people died didn't faze him. Where people killed did. He was an old hand at telling himself it wasn't anything. He knew how to reassure himself. Through the years, he'd managed to shake off most of the heebie-jeebies. He would concentrate on the work. The work, he said, is nothing more than cleaning up a big old mess. He would stop himself before he said it was like cleaning up after a big party. That was in poor taste.

He knew it was all about Clorox and detergent and Pine-Sol and alcohol. He broke down and hosed off and carted out biological matter. He was about elbow grease and scrubbing. It was as simple as that. It was as simple as out, out, damned spot. He knew there was nothing to get the willies over. And yet...

Maxwell would clean a death place, and he would get the sense he was accompanied. It wasn't ghosts, exactly. It was more like emotions. He would sometimes feel emotions breeze across his skin or tap him on the shoulder. He could never place who owned the emotions, or exactly which emotions they were. They had no context. They simply were. It was odd, he knew.

Later, sometimes, when he ate a meal or drove in his car, he also felt accompanied. He would get a very quick, small and specific flashback of a cleanup job in a death place, and would feel the emotions all over again.

He stopped and almost retched. Then he picked up a piece of gooey flesh with a pair of tongs and put it in a garbage bag. It was about the size of a plum. At times like this, he imagined chewing on a small piece of foil, or Brillo, and that would distract him. He had started by imagining sucking on a lemon, but that wore out a long time ago. He placed the piece of flesh under some old Handi-Wipes in the red biohazard bag so he wouldn't come across it again accidentally.

He wondered if he would be asked to fix the bullet holes. That could run into serious money—up to $10,000. He was doing the cleanup for $5,000. He charged them extra because Doris Lambert didn't meet his eye. She just paid him and got away from him. *I wonder who that belonged to?* Maxwell thought suddenly about the small piece of person he was lugging around in the red plastic garbage bag as he crossed the restaurant to get a fresh bucket. *I wonder what that was?*

❦

It's not anger, Maxwell thought as he coiled up the cord from the steam cleaner. *I don't sense anger here. There was probably no anger at Treblinka.*

He imagined he was one of the victims in the restaurant, *one of my victims. That's bad. I can't do that, I shouldn't do that,* he thought. *Who am I to put myself in their place?*

He thought about how the shooting was less than two days before and the sun was out and the place was filled with people. He imagined the hum of voices, the

225

annoying bleeps of video games. Okay, you're eating, Maxwell thought as he sat at a table and faced the entrance. You're eating pizza, or a sandwich. You're not thinking about much. And then...what? The guy starts to shoot?

All right. You do what? Why is he shooting? You hit the deck. Bam, on the floor. Where? He looked around. His perspective was all messed up on the floor. Nothing, he realized, was clear to these poor people. There's a guy shooting. Is he shooting at me? Is he shooting me next? No. No one thinks they're next. Is he mad at only one person? Is there only one person doing the shooting? Is it a shootout with the police? Is this guy a bank robber? Just what in the hell is going on?

Jesus. Too much.

Maxwell got up. He felt a little foolish about his exercise to see what it's like to get shot.

So sad, he thought. He wanted to leave the restaurant and get back to Phoenix before the morning traffic started in. I hate it. This is the last job, Maxwell said to himself. He always said that after a murder cleanup. But the money was good, and he was building a reputation. Business, these days, was booming. I wonder if this job will bring referrals?

It was so desperate in here the other day, he thought as he stood near the front door one last time.

We sometimes wonder "Where will I die?" Maxwell thought. No one thinks "the Pizza Man." It makes no sense. I didn't miss a spot, did I? Maybe I should walk through one more time. Nah. It's clean. If not, they know where to reach me.

This guy, Sam Tryor. He walked in right here. He stood in this exact spot at one point, maybe, and said to himself, "I'll take the gun out and start shooting now." Why?

For six shattering steps, Maxwell walked in my shoes. He walked from the entrance into the restaurant. He held his arms as though he were holding a gun. He walked along. Bang, bang. Pretending. Bang, bang. To shoot people.

Could I do something like this? he thought. Maybe they were not nice people. Maybe they deserved it. Bang, bang, bang. Maybe they were terrible, terrible people. What makes someone do this, even if they *were* terrible? I guess the police will find out.

This is so messed up. This is nuts. It's so sad. Maybe Sam Tryor was sad, and he took it out on these poor people. Hoping they won't get shot. Hoping they won't die. We all die, only not today, they thought, not at the Pizza Man, not like this.

In his mind, Maxwell saw them as they scrambled along the floor, scratched along the walls, yelled, cried. He felt power as the gunman, yes, he did. He was accompanied then.

Then he felt sick. He became overwhelmed, and he had to go outside.

The night air was a sweet slap back to normality. Maxwell smelled the rain. The creosote bushes in the desert blossomed and brought that scent, that aroma you only find in Arizona. It smells so nice, and feels so nice, he thought.

He looked back at the restaurant, got a chill and went back in to finish up.

He hauled his gear to his van. He locked up, stood on the sidewalk and looked at the mounds of bouquets, stuffed animals and other offerings stacked in front of the restaurant. He dragged the white garbage bags to the Dumpster and the red biohazard ones to his van. Some had blood and others had fist-sized pieces of people in them. There were fingernails and pens and dentures and an empty wallet and two neckties and five different shoes in those bags. Did they want me to take the flowers or leave the flowers? Maxwell wondered. Usually, he took the flowers to a nursing home for the old people. What did they say? The news conference, he remembered. There might be another news conference, so leave the flowers for that.

This is a desperate place. How desperate do you have to be, killing all those people? What did they ever do to anyone? I'm sure they were all good people. I'm so sure. So sad.

Maxwell bent down and gathered the stuffed animals. They'd told him about the flowers, but they didn't say anything about the stuffed animals. He thought the Salvation Army would find kids who would love to have them.

He got in his van and drove. He was relieved to leave the area and the town. He vowed five times on the way home that he would never do a murder cleanup again. *Not ever. Never. No more for me. Too much. These poor people. I could never. Nope. Never. But the money's so good.*

—16—

I have one more ghost story for you.

Sam Tryor was fifty-two years old when he walked into a restaurant in Sierra Vista, Arizona, on Memorial Day and shot forty people before he killed himself. He came back for two days and haunted his brother, a cop, a reporter and some other people who tried to find out why he did what he did.

Sam didn't know at first who he was, much less why he did it. He was a ghost who was along for the ride. He found out he was just a regular guy, the same as anyone you might pass on the street. He grew up in Detroit, came out to Arizona, and pulled a hitch in the Army. His service was unspectacular. All he got from it was a joke he liked to make. He would fake a limp, pat his thigh and say, "Yeah, it's my Cold War wound."

He was married and divorced. He ran his own business. He killed forty people for no apparent reason then blew his brains out.

After that, even his haunting was unremarkable. He told a cop the name of a song the cop had stuck in his head. He made his brother turn on a lamp. He decided there was one thing worse than doing what he did, and that was to not even want to know why.

He remembered why he shot all those people and his ghost went away.

◦═◦

I remember now. I didn't think about philosophy or reasons, or life or death. I thought about logistics and actions. I concentrated on getting through it. Except for a couple of stray thoughts, that was what was on my mind when I shot those people. Then, in the final three seconds of my life, I realized why I did it, and it made sense to me.

Harry Bronsky gave me his guns to hold on to because he was on probation. It was an AK-47 and a .45-caliber automatic. I was on my way home and stopped at the Pizza Man. I had the guns in a gym bag and grabbed the bag because there were no locks on my truck and I didn't want anyone to steal Harry's guns.

I got a slice of pizza, sat down and moved the bag because it looked like it might fall off the table. First, before I touched it, I looked inside to make sure the safeties were on. Then, when I went to move it...

It just went off, like *oops*. The first shot hit solid and sent a guy cutting pizza for his son into a wall.

"Wow," I said. "I'm sorry."

I had no idea how it happened. I apologized, but I was confused. I apologized in the same tone a mother uses when she tells her child the hamster died.

"What was that?" someone said. "What the hell?"

I looked at the AK-47. A woman went over to the man who had been shot. She looked at me with an expression like the saleslady in the china shop about to say, *You know you have to pay for that now, don't you?* The child with them—he couldn't have been more than four—put a bite of pizza into his mouth and looked at the man. He clapped his hands like he was saying *goody-goody gumdrops!*

230

There was movement. Chairs scraped against the floor.

"Okay," I said, grasping what had happened. "It's all okay."

Sounds gained momentum and built on one another. Very quickly, it got incredibly noisy. I had never heard anything like it.

"All right now," I said. I talked only for my own benefit, but I didn't know it. No one could hear me. "It's fine."

A wall of noise and panic moved in on me. There were screams. The man who had been shot slapped the floor with a flat open hand. He kicked the table leg with his heel. Silverware went flying across tabletops.

"Mike," the wife whispered. Then she yelled "Mike!" over and over while another woman, a large one in a yellow flower-print sundress, grabbed her purse, put it in the bend of her elbow and started running. She had one hand over her mouth.

I felt vibrations from the floor. I felt it through the soles of my feet.

"Mike!" the woman yelled, "Oh my God Mike oh my God."

I yelled, but no one heard me over the noise and the awakening to the reality of what was going on.

"All right. Okay. All right now," I said.

That's when I fired. I fired multiple shots in a line. It was a dotted line that started in the center of the woman in the yellow sundress and led away from her. She went down. Her purse trailed after her. The man next to her was shot in the throat.

It was amazing. It was amazing that it was happening and that the gun was in my hand. Even more amazing was that it felt correct for me to be doing this. I wasn't angry. I wasn't thinking about anything except what I was doing. It simply felt like what I should do.

That feeling scared me, but I didn't have any time to consider it.

A kid in a corduroy baseball cap looked at me. He held his right ear and just stood there with his mouth open. At first, he didn't move to protect anyone, not even himself. Then he turned to get out of there and tell someone about it.

"Don't leave," I told him.

I kept on firing. I heard shell casings drop to the floor with hollow clinks.

"Don't," I said.

More people fell. Some staggered forward from the impact of bullets then fell. Others just sank. It was crazy. I walked a few steps and realized I had a body, that I was alive and this was happening. It was like my legs were numb or asleep, and I wanted to wake them up.

"God, I'm sweating," I said.

I ran for the door and got in front of it. I had to block it. Again, logistics.

"No," I said. "Okay. Okay."

I put my arm around the shoulder of the kid who had held his ear.

"Go and sit down now," I said to him, as gently as I could. "Everybody, listen. I want everybody to just listen."

Everybody huddled in two groups in the corners about twenty feet away. They moved chairs in front of them and held on to table legs for protection. One woman said "Hail, Mary." Another said, "Mike, wake up."

"It's all right now," I assured them.

I always had trouble talking in front of groups. I preferred the one-on-one.

"Is there anyone in the back there?" I asked the kid in the baseball cap. "Go check. Go. You."

It took the young man three tries to open the swinging half-door to the kitchen.

"Pull it," I told him. "Try pulling it. That's the stuff. Good."

There was heavy breathing. Everything in the room was becoming less fuzzy. I was really in it. I saw strangers look at one another to confirm what was happening was really happening. The two clumps of people huddled tighter together and looked at the gun. They didn't look at me—I was obscured by the greater reality of the gun.

I didn't know what to do. I just stood there.

"He's alive," someone screamed.

"No one's back there," the kid said in a twisted yell once he came back from the kitchen. "Can I go now? I'd like to go. Now. I'll just..."

And he left.

There is very little time left, I thought.

The first guy who was shot was still hitting the floor with his hand. It was soft as a whisper. Slap, slap, slap.

It got very quiet then, and I thought it was fascinating how everybody shared so completely in the event. I looked out a window that had the blinds up, the only one where I could see out. The sunny day continued. The cars passed by on Fry Boulevard. The tires made that sizzling sound.

"Do something," said a woman in the corner next to her boyfriend. "Do something, Jerry. Look at him."

She wanted him to be a hero. That was a mistake.

Jerry got up and made it only three steps before I shot him in the chest. A smattering of goo hit the window with a splat. Behind the balls of blood, I saw a guy in the parking lot get out of his car. I saw him look at the restaurant window. Time was getting even shorter.

"I got to do it," I said.

I thought about Sharon Baskin and her husband Fred. I was introduced to them at a party when I was stationed in Virginia. I just had to meet them because they were the nicest people and I would love them.

She worked for a credit card company that had been fined for charging poor people huge interest rates and fees. Sharon was relieved because the fine against the company was small, and it wouldn't hurt the company. Fred was a marketing guy for a cigarette company. He said it was a great job because cigarettes sold themselves. They were nice people. What the hell?

I braced the gun against my shoulder and kept it low while I walked and fired. People scattered, and a few hit the ground. One man with blond hair and a chain that held his wallet to his belt loop crouched behind the dead woman in the yellow sundress and called for his mother.

I straight-line walked and shot on automatic. It was very easy. The clip emptied. I had another. I reloaded and continued until I was about five feet from the wall.

"Oh, damn," I said.

I turned around to the other group of people and shot a college girl as she ran for the door. She wore a T-shirt, bathing suit bottoms and flip-flops. When she fell the flip-flops slapped against her heel one last time and that was it.

People dove under tables. They kicked and hurled their bodies into tight places. They scratched along the Mexican-tiled floor. It was very fast. Everyone moved very fast.

I remembered a statistic. In 1970, seventy-nine percent of students said their goal in college was to develop a meaningful philosophy of life. In 2005, seventy-five percent of students in college said their primary objective was to be financially very well off.

"Hot bullets," I said.

I stopped at a table and poured a Pepsi on the top of the gun, and on my hand. I had no idea why I did that. I stopped firing and watched a man—the same man who had been looking in earlier—behind the wheel of a car in the parking lot. His hand slipped along the gearshift as he put it in reverse. He was horrified, looking into the restaurant, but he was still a careful driver—he checked his mirrors before he backed up.

He was sure to call someone. They would come soon.

I adjusted my grip on the gun. I felt like crying. I gripped the gun and sucked in as hard as a long-jumper before a leap. Then I just went everywhere with the gun. The barrel flying hot, shots opened along the wall, glass shattered, an upper arm got all chewed up, and the cash register got hit. Its drawer popped open like a tongue. I raised my foot high and kicked it, hard. Nickels, dimes, quarters and pennies sprinkled down. Bills fluttered. They looked absurd in the smoke, and looked weirder still when they landed. One $20 bill soaked up the blood on a hole in the college girl's forehead.

"He's a mess," Jerry's girlfriend said. She was on the floor holding him as he spasmed. His shirt was reddened wounds. "This is a mess." The woman stroked his head and muttered, "Jerry, do something. Do something, Jerry, do something."

I thought: Hooters makes $1 billion a year.

God, I was tired all of a sudden.

I raised the gun to fire and everyone tensed, but I didn't shoot. I dropped down to relax. I thrust my arm with the gun forward. I wanted to shake it off me, get rid of it. Then I did, and it clattered to the ground, empty. I looked around, picked up an iced tea and took a long gulp.

"I always liked iced tea," I said.

No one moved when I spoke. A lot of people kept their eyes on the gun, even though it was on the floor. For a few moments, everyone was quiet and still. It was like the silence when no one can think of what to say at a party.

"Looks like a bad day for the home team," I said. I smiled. I opened my mouth, and it was so dry it made a huge sound. I knew what I had to do.

I pulled the .45 from my back pocket, and I put the barrel in my mouth.

My life flashed before my eyes, and I was happy to get that over with.

"Oh, yes, finally, you fuck," a voice said.

I looked toward the ceiling. An overhead fan spun slowly. I took the gun from my mouth and aimed it around. I didn't shoot.

"Come on," someone said.

Ten feet away, a black woman stood up, walked to the door and said, "Let me. I'll do it if you can't."

"No, that's fine," I said. "Thank you. I can take care of it. I can."

"All right, then," the woman said.

The other people started moving.

"Don't," I said. "Don't move."

They weren't listening.

It was so sunny out. It was a good day. I put the tip of the gun to my mouth.

"Bad day for the home team," I said. "I'm sorry about all this."

〇〜〇

I should have said it out loud—it might have made what happened in the days afterward different.

Instead, I was thinking.

Concentrate the hate we are exposed to for no reason every day.

Concentrate the powerlessness that people feel over their own lives every day.

Concentrate the meanness and mistrust and incivility that people feel and express casually to one another every day.

Concentrate the sense of loss people cannot explain but live with, and do nothing about, every day.

Concentrate the effort as they try and fail to make some sense of it, or at least get out from under it, as it crushes them every day.

Concentrate it all down to one moment and one person, and you have me with a gun in my hand for three minutes.

I pulled the trigger.

END

ABOUT THE AUTHOR

This is ALEX O'MEARA's first novel. He lives in Bisbee, Arizona.

ABOUT THE ARTIST

CHRIS CARTWRIGHT is a computer artist who uses 3D programs and paint programs to create her works. Although she creates covers for any type of story, her favorites are fantasy, sci-fi and horror. She originally became interested in web design, which she went to school for, but after taking some art classes, found a new passion. Besides Zumaya, Chris has also created covers for *Apex Digest*, Outskirts Press, *Penwomanship*, *Whispers of Wickedness*, *Midnight Street*, *Insidious Reflections* and many other publishers and authors.

If you are a writer or publisher and are in need of a cover artist or illustrator, you may contact Chris at digitellart@yahoo.com or visit her websites at: http://www.digitelldesign.com

LaVergne, TN USA
05 October 2010
199678LV00001B/19/P